Sinners

The Screenplay

Sourabh Mukherjee

Ukiyoto Publishing

All global publishing rights are held by

Ukiyoto Publishing

Published in 2023

Content Copyright © Sourabh Mukherjee

ISBN 9789358465297

All rights reserved.

No part of this publication may be reproduced, transmitted, or stored in a retrieval system, in any form by any means, electronic, mechanical, photocopying, recording or otherwise, without the prior permission of the publisher.

The moral rights of the author have been asserted.

This is a work of fiction. Names, characters, businesses, places, events, locales, and incidents are either the products of the author's imagination or used in a fictitious manner. Any resemblance to actual persons, living or dead, or actual events is purely coincidental.

This book is sold subject to the condition that it shall not by way of trade or otherwise, be lent, resold, hired out or otherwise circulated, without the publisher's prior consent, in any form of binding or cover other than that in which it is published.

www.ukiyoto.com

Contents

Introductory Scene	1
Act 1	3
Act 2	8
Act 3	10
Act 4	14
Act 5	19
Act 6	23
Act 7	30
Act 8	34
Act 9	39
Act 10	41
Act 11	45
Act 12	48
Act 13	52
Act 14	54
Act 15	57
Act 16	65
Act 17	70
Act 18	75
Act 19	77
Act 20	82
Act 21	86
Act 22	88
Act 23	93
Act 24	95
Act 25	97
Act 26	99
Act 27	102

Act 28	104
Act 29	111
Act 30	114
Act 31	121
Act 32	124
Act 33	127
Act 34	129
Act 35	131
Act 36	135
Act 37	140
Act 38	142
Act 39	145
Act 40	147
Act 41	149
Act 42	152
Act 43	157
Act 44	161
Act 45	163
Act 46	167
Act 47	172
Act 48	174
Act 49	177
Act 50	180
Act 51	182
Act 52	184
Act 53	189
Act 54	192
Final Scene	194

Introductory Scene

EXT. PRESTIGE APARTMENTS - BANDRA, MUMBAI - NIGHT

The atmosphere is chaotic. The noise of cars honking and people shouting fills the air. The drizzling rain adds to the frenzy. The bright city lights reflect off the wet roads, creating a shimmering effect.

CLOSE UP on a police barricade. Behind it, a sea of photographers and reporters push and shove, trying to get the best angle. Flashbulbs pop, momentarily blinding the police officers trying to maintain order.

PAN across the crowd, capturing the various faces - some professional, some merely curious. The long lenses of press photographers compete with the mobile cameras of bystanders.

ZOOM OUT to reveal the grandeur of the thirty-storeyed Prestige Apartments. Its entrance is sealed off, guarded by more police officers.

CUT TO a series of television vans parked along the road, satellite dishes pointing skyward. Journalists stand in front of cameras, delivering their pieces to camera with animated expressions.

JOURNALIST 1
"...he was found inside his penthouse apartment, his wrist slashed..."

JOURNALIST 2
"...we don't know yet if he was alone when he died..."

JOURNALIST 3
"...forensic experts are inside his apartment..."

CUT TO a close-up of the building's nameplate: "Prestige Apartments."

INT. PENTHOUSE - PRESTIGE APARTMENTS - NIGHT

The room is dimly lit. The glow from a television screen casts eerie shadows. The volume is loud, perhaps a news channel discussing the very incident unfolding.

PAN across the lavish living room to reveal VIKRAM OBEROI, lifeless, sprawled on a plush sofa. His wrist is slashed, blood staining the rich fabric.

CLOSE UP on an empty whiskey glass, glistening with condensation. Next to it, a bottle, more than half empty.

PAN DOWN to the floor, where a kitchen knife, smeared with blood, lies on the plush carpet.

FADE OUT.

Act 1

Four months ago

INT. NEXGEN TECHNOLOGIES LOBBY - HI-TECH PARK, ANDHERI - MORNING

The lobby of NexGen Technologies is buzzing with activity. Employees, dressed in formal attire, hurry about, ready to start their workday. The grandeur of the imposing tower is evident, with its sleek design and modern aesthetics.

CLOSE UP on the bank of elevators. A long queue has formed, and employees wait impatiently.

PAN to SONAL VERMA as she rushes to join the queue. Her hair is tied back in a neat ponytail, silver hoops dangle from her ears, and her glossy lips shimmer. She wears a fitted purple shirt and black pants that showcase her figure.

CUT TO various men in the queue, sneaking glances at Sonal. Some adjust their ties, run their fingers through their hair, or subtly suck in their tummies. Whispers and murmurs fill the air.

FLASHBACK:

INT. SONAL'S BEDROOM - DAY

Sonal sits surrounded by a pile of dog-eared books. A convocation photograph shows a younger, more hopeful Sonal. She clutches a degree in commerce.

CUT TO a series of quick shots: Sonal filling out job applications, attending interviews, facing lecherous supervisors, and receiving meagre paychecks.

FLASHBACK END.

INT. NEXGEN TECHNOLOGIES LOBBY - MORNING

Back in the present, Sonal stands tall, proud of her position at NexGen. The company logo is prominently displayed, symbolizing its growing dominance in the tech market.

CUT TO a poster showcasing NexGen's latest smartphone. The tagline reads: "State-of-the-Art Technology at Affordable Prices."

PAN to VIKRAM OBEROI's photograph on a wall, labelled "Vice President - India Operations." He's strikingly handsome, with bright eyes, a sharp nose, and a chiselled jawline. His unruly hair adds to his allure.

FLASHBACK:

INT. NEXGEN TECHNOLOGIES INDUCTION HALL - DAY

New recruits, including Sonal, sit in neat rows. Vikram Oberoi stands at the podium, addressing them. Sonal is visibly smitten, hanging on to his every word.

CUT TO PRACHI, an experienced HR executive, whispering to Sonal.

PRACHI
"He is married. And the wife is quite a looker herself."

Sonal's face falls slightly, but she tries to hide her disappointment.

> FLASHBACK END.

> INT. NEXGEN TECHNOLOGIES LOBBY - MORNING

The elevator doors open, and Sonal steps in, stealing one last glance at Vikram's photograph before the doors close.

> INT. NEXGEN TECHNOLOGIES CAFETERIA - MORNING

Sonal and Prachi sit at a table, sipping their morning coffee. The cafeteria is bustling with employees chatting and laughing.

SONAL
"Oh, the best ones are always taken, aren't they?"

PRACHI
(smiling)

"Well, truth be told, our man doesn't score high on commitment. Can't stay away from temptations."

Sonal raises an eyebrow, intrigued.

SONAL
"Really? With a gorgeous wife tucked away?"

PRACHI
"Don't be fooled by the photographs from the office parties. It's all a sham!"

SONAL
(sceptically)
"The wife doesn't know?"

PRACHI
(winking)
"Or, our man is too smart to show."

INT. NEXGEN TECHNOLOGIES ADMINISTRATION BLOCK - DAY

Sonal sits at her desk, working diligently. The Administration block is a hive of activity, with employees busy at their tasks.

PAN to Vikram's corner office. Its glass walls offer a clear view inside. Vikram is on a call, but his gaze frequently drifts towards Sonal.

CUT TO Sonal, who can't help but glance back at Vikram every so often.

INT. NEXGEN TECHNOLOGIES PANTRY - DAY

Vikram stands by the coffee machine, pouring himself a cup. Sonal enters, holding her coffee mug. They exchange pleasantries, their conversation casual yet filled with underlying tension.

MONTAGE:

Sonal and Vikram chatting in the pantry.
The two of them sharing a table in the cafeteria, laughing over lunch.
Vikram and Sonal stepping out for a quick afternoon coffee break.

INT. NEXGEN TECHNOLOGIES ADMINISTRATION BLOCK - DAY

Employees whisper and exchange glances as Sonal and Vikram walk by, their camaraderie evident. Sonal doesn't seem to care about the gossip.

CUT TO AARTI BANSAL, Vikram's secretary. She watches the duo with a mix of disdain and jealousy. Her displeasure is evident.

Act 2

INT. AARTI'S ONE-BEDROOM FLAT - EVENING

The ambiance is moody. Raindrops patter against the window, and the distant rumble of thunder can be heard. The room is dimly lit by a single lamp on a study desk. Outside, the wet roads reflect the glow of streetlights.

AARTI stands near the window, looking out at the rain. VIKRAM is a few steps behind her, a look of concern on his face.

AARTI
(voice filled with emotion)
"I've been missing you, Vikram. When we finally meet after so long, all we do is fight."

She tries to move away, but VIKRAM attempts to pull her close. She resists, distancing herself.

AARTI
"I know about her, Vikram. The new girl in the office."

VIKRAM
(raising his hands defensively)
"Aarti, it's not what you think."

AARTI
(teary-eyed)

"Everyone knows about us, Vikram. I hate the whispers, the stares. I thought this was just a fling, but it's more for me now."

VIKRAM
"We're in this together, Aarti. You're getting it all wrong."

AARTI's emotions bubble over, tears spilling from her eyes.

AARTI
"I'm so confused, Vikram. I see you with Sonal and it kills me inside."

They share another passionate kiss, their emotions raw and palpable. AARTI pushes VIKRAM onto the couch, her actions aggressive and desperate. As she begins to unbuckle his belt, VIKRAM's expression changes subtly.

CLOSE UP on VIKRAM's face. Although he's with AARTI, his thoughts are clearly elsewhere.

VIKRAM
(voiceover)
Sonal...

Act 3

INT. MARRIOTT RENAISSANCE - ELEVATOR - NIGHT

The elevator doors open, revealing VIKRAM and SONAL. Vikram, with a hint of mischief in his eyes, places his hand on the small of Sonal's back, guiding her out.

INT. MARRIOTT RENAISSANCE - RESTAURANT - NIGHT

The ambiance is romantic. Soft piano music fills the air, and dim lights create a cozy atmosphere. Red candles and fresh rose buds adorn the tables.

VIKRAM leads SONAL to a reserved table in a corner, overlooking the serene Powai Lake. As they sit, Sonal takes in the surroundings, her heart racing.

A WAITER approaches, lighting the red candle on their table. Sonal's gaze shifts to Vikram, who's been watching her intently.

VIKRAM
(smiling)
"You seem lost. Everything alright?"

SONAL
(smiling back)
"Just that... all this feels like a dream."

VIKRAM

"That's what it is, Sonal. A dream. And we're living it right now."

He places his hand over hers, their connection palpable.

SONAL
"Such a lovely place! Do you come here often?"

VIKRAM
(laughing)
"Not really. I usually go to bars when I'm alone. But tonight is special."

Sonal blushes at his words.

The WAITER returns with a wine list. Vikram orders a Chardonnay for both.

After a short while, the WAITER returns, presenting the wine bottle to Vikram for approval. Vikram nods, and the waiter pours a bit into Sonal's glass. She takes a sip, trying to mimic the actions of a wine connoisseur, which makes both of them stifle their laughter.

INT. MARRIOTT RENAISSANCE - RESTAURANT - NIGHT

The table is adorned with empty wine glasses and plates with remnants of dessert. The ambiance is still romantic, but there's a more relaxed atmosphere between VIKRAM and SONAL.

VIKRAM
"You know, I've never felt this way before."

SONAL
(smiling)
"Neither have I."

Their conversation is interrupted by the buzz of Vikram's phone. Sonal's face tenses up, wondering if it's his wife.

VIKRAM
(on the phone)
"Hey chief, how's it going? ... I'm at a restaurant... Anything urgent? ... Alright, I'll call you back in an hour."

He hangs up and looks at Sonal apologetically.

VIKRAM
"That was Dev, my boss. I need to call him back in an hour. I'm sorry, but we need to leave."

INT. VIKRAM'S CAR - NIGHT

The car stops in front of Sonal's house. The atmosphere inside is thick with emotion.

SONAL
"Thanks for the lovely evening, Vikram. I'll always remember this."

VIKRAM leans in, giving her a soft kiss.

VIKRAM

(winking)
"I will too. And I hope for many more evenings like this."

SONAL
(laughing)
"Get back to work! Dev must be waiting."

She gives him a quick peck on the cheek and exits the car, her red dress catching Vikram's eye as she walks away.

VIKRAM
(to himself, smiling)
"Aarti Bansal is history."

He starts the car and drives away.

Act 4

INT. DEV'S LUXURIOUS HOME OFFICE - NIGHT

The room is filled with awards, mementos, and photos from Dev's long career. A large desk sits in the middle, with a state-of-the-art computer setup. The walls are adorned with framed articles about NexGen's success and a few from Dev's time at Alpha Tech.

NARRATOR (V.O.)
"Devesh Nair, known as 'Dev', was the brain behind NexGen. After thirty years at Alpha Tech, he left to chase his dream."

Flashback sequences show:

INT. ALPHA TECH BOARDROOM - DAY (FLASHBACK)

Dev passionately presents his innovative business plans to a room full of executives. They seem disinterested, some even dismissive.

NARRATOR (V.O.)
"His ideas were revolutionary, but they fell on deaf ears."

INT. COFFEE SHOP - DAY (FLASHBACK)

Dev sits across from ASHOK PANDEY, his old friend. They're deep in conversation, with Dev sketching out ideas on a napkin.

NARRATOR (V.O.)
"But with the support of his old friend Ashok, NexGen was born."

INT. NEXGEN RESEARCH LAB - DAY (FLASHBACK)

Scientists and engineers work on cutting-edge gadgets. The atmosphere is buzzing with innovation.

NARRATOR (V.O.)
"NexGen was the future. Affordable, innovative, and ahead of its time."

INT. DEV'S LUXURIOUS HOME OFFICE - NIGHT

Back to the present. Dev sits at his desk, looking at the latest market survey results. His expression is one of concern.

NARRATOR (V.O.)
"But the last few quarters had been challenging. The market was shifting, and Dev knew he had to act."

Dev's phone rings. He sees VIKRAM's name on the caller ID and answers immediately.

DEV
(with a hint of sarcasm)
"Vikram, the quarterly results are out. We aren't the giants we once were."

VIKRAM (V.O.)

"Are we declaring this week?"

DEV
"We are. And we need a plan, Vikram. Our shareholders deserve answers."

INT. VIKRAM'S LIVING ROOM - NIGHT

The room is dimly lit. Vikram sits on a plush sofa, phone pressed to his ear. He's visibly tense, occasionally rubbing his temples. On a nearby table, a glass of whiskey sits untouched.

VIKRAM
"Yes, Dev, I understand the gravity of the situation."

DEV (V.O.)
"The market's talking, Vikram. They think our golden days are behind us. We need to act, and act fast."

VIKRAM
"I've been considering a merger with Quantum Technologies in Japan. It could be the boost we need."

DEV (V.O.)
"That's a start. But our survey results show we're losing the youth. We need to get them back."

Vikram takes a deep breath, gathering his thoughts.

VIKRAM

"I've been working on a plan. We're looking at a partnership with Evita."

DEV (V.O.)
(confused)
"The clothing line? How does that tie in with our tech?"

VIKRAM
"It's about blending fashion with technology. I'll present the full plan tomorrow."

There's a pause. Vikram can almost hear the gears turning in Dev's head.

DEV (V.O.)
"I'm intrigued. Let's discuss this in detail tomorrow."

VIKRAM
"Understood, Dev."

DEV (V.O.)
"Remember, Vikram, a few more quarters like this, and we're done. Alpha is right on our heels. We can't afford to slip."

VIKRAM
"I'm on it, Dev. I'll set up meetings with Evita and push for a swift collaboration."

DEV (V.O.)
"Good. Get some rest. We have a big day tomorrow."

The call ends. Vikram sets the phone down, lost in thought. He glances at his watch, contemplating.

VIKRAM
(to himself)
"Is it too late to call Sonal?"

Act 5

INT. DEV'S OFFICE - MORNING

The room is spacious and modern, with large windows allowing sunlight to stream in. Dev sits behind a sleek desk, while Vikram stands in front of it, holding a tablet with some designs and data. Both men are in business attire, looking sharp and focused.

VIKRAM
(excitedly)
"Dev, smart wearables! They're the future!"

DEV
(raising an eyebrow)
"Explain."

VIKRAM
"Imagine garments or accessories with embedded tech, like sensors and displays..."

DEV
(interrupting)
"Cut the tech talk. Give me something tangible."

VIKRAM
(thinking for a moment)
"Alright. Picture a cyclist wearing a denim jacket. Looks ordinary, right? But with a touch on its cuff, he can change music tracks, answer calls, or access navigation."

DEV
(nods)

"Go on."

VIKRAM
"Or a backpack that changes colors based on body temperature or sunlight. Or a coat with hidden heating technology, adjusting to the outside weather."

DEV
(impressed)
"So, it's beyond the usual smartwatches and fitness bands?"

VIKRAM
"Exactly. It's the next level. But here's the catch: these products need to be fashionable. They need to look good. Tech companies often miss that mark."

DEV
"So, you're saying we need a fashion touch?"

VIKRAM
(smiling)
"That's where Evita comes in. We provide the tech, they provide the style. Together, we create products that aren't just smart but also desirable."

DEV
(leaning back)
"And you believe this is the game-changer?"

VIKRAM
"Absolutely. It's not just about the tech. It's about creating something people want to wear. That's the key."

INT. DEV'S OFFICE - MORNING

The room remains bathed in sunlight, with the atmosphere now more charged with excitement. Dev leans forward, intrigued by Vikram's proposal, while Vikram, filled with enthusiasm, continues to explain.

DEV
"So, what's the plan with Evita?"

VIKRAM
(leaning in)
"We collaborate. Their designers, our tech experts. Together, we create these fashionable smart wearables. And then, we hit the market. Fashion shows, ads everywhere. We'll be unstoppable."

DEV
(raising an eyebrow)
"And you think this hasn't been tried before?"

VIKRAM
(pause)
"It has. Especially by Alpha. But our partnership offer? It's something Evita won't be able to turn down."

DEV
(skeptically)
"Who's handling this?"

VIKRAM
(smiling confidently)

"Ashwin. He's on it. We're in good hands."

DEV
(nods)
"Alright. But we need to be flexible. If we need to make concessions to seal this deal, we should be ready."

VIKRAM
"Understood, Dev. You'll have the proposal in your inbox by tomorrow. We're crafting an offer they simply can't refuse."

Act 6

INT. NEXGEN OFFICE - NIGHT

The office is dimly lit, with only a few overhead lights on. Computer monitors cast a soft glow. The room is mostly empty, save for AGASTYA, a young engineer with a slightly disheveled appearance. He's surrounded by pizza boxes, soda cans, and the remnants of a long workday. The hum of computers and the distant sound of traffic are the only noises.

Agastya's phone buzzes, breaking the silence. He glances at the screen, seeing a "PRIVATE NUMBER" displayed. Hesitating for a moment, he answers on the third ring.

AGASTYA:
Hello?

MYSTERIOUS VOICE (V.O.):
Is this Agastya Bakshi?

AGASTYA:
Yes… who's this?

MYSTERIOUS VOICE (V.O.):
Agastya, my apologies for calling you late. I assure you this won't take too long. But, we need to talk in private. Where are you right now?

Agastya looks around, noting the emptiness of the office.

AGASTYA:
I'm at work, but we can talk. Not too many people around at this time of the night.

MYSTERIOUS VOICE (V.O.):
Great! Then let's talk business. I belong to a private investigation agency that's currently looking into the dealings of the company you are working for. There are reports of certain financial irregularities in the business.

Agastya sits up, alarmed.

AGASTYA:
What - what do you want from me? I work in Network and Systems. I don't think you have the right number!

MYSTERIOUS VOICE (V.O.):
Agastya, I know who I am talking to. We need access to the e-mail accounts of some of the top guys in your company to check their correspondences. And I've been told that you are the right man for the job.

Agastya takes a sip from his flat cola, trying to process the information.

AGASTYA:
Why - why me? You can speak to my Manager in the morning. He -

MYSTERIOUS VOICE (V.O.):
Agastya, this is a covert operation and we are a private agency. We cannot turn up at your office with an order to gain access to

these accounts. Also, right now, we're not sure how many of the big guys are involved and in what ways. For all you know, your boss might as well be a party! Let's not forget that, he has access to all records of transactions. We do not want anyone getting alert and tampering with the data we are looking for. We cannot risk exposure. It'll take us some time to complete the basic investigation. And I'd really appreciate your cooperation while we are at it. Once we have enough evidence at our disposal, we will make this official.

INT. NEXGEN OFFICE - NIGHT

Agastya sits in his chair, deep in thought, the weight of the conversation pressing down on him. The dim light from his computer screen casts a glow on his face.

AGASTYA (V.O.):
Could this be a hoax?

MYSTERIOUS VOICE (V.O.):
One of my agents will get in touch with you. You'll be working with her. We want to win your trust.

Agastya hesitates, his fingers drumming on the desk.

AGASTYA:
How do I trust you? What's in it for me?

MYSTERIOUS VOICE (V.O.):

We'll compensate for your time and cooperation. You'll have no reason to complain about the money.

Visions of his new car and the advertisement for the apartment complex in South Mumbai flash in Agastya's mind. The allure of financial freedom is tempting.

MYSTERIOUS VOICE (V.O.):
So, we're good to go here, right?

AGASTYA:
Well...

Before he can finish, the voice interrupts.

MYSTERIOUS VOICE (V.O.):
Thanks for your cooperation, Agastya. Ruchika will get in touch with you shortly.

The call ends abruptly. Agastya stares at his phone, a mix of anxiety and curiosity evident on his face. He contemplates calling someone but decides against it.

AGASTYA (V.O.):
I can always step back if things go south. Maybe even report the guy.

His phone buzzes, snapping him out of his thoughts. A Whatsapp message notification pops up. It's from Ruchika.

RUCHIKA (TEXT):
Hey, this is Ruchika.

AGASTYA (TEXT):
Hi.

RUCHIKA (TEXT):
My boss spoke to you a while ago. I thought I'd introduce myself. I'll be working with you.

Agastya adds the number to his contacts. Ruchika's display picture appears, and Agastya is taken aback by her beauty.

AGASTYA (V.O.):
Wow... She's... stunning.

               INT. NEXGEN OFFICE - NIGHT

Agastya's phone continues to buzz with notifications. The dim light from his computer screen illuminates his face, which now has a hint of a smile.

AGASTYA (TEXT):
Great to connect.

RUCHIKA (TEXT):
Likewise, Agastya. Working late?

AGASTYA (TEXT):
Yes. This is pretty much my schedule these days.

RUCHIKA (TEXT):
Too bad.

AGASTYA (TEXT):

Hey, looks like I'm not the only one burning midnight oil...you are working too!

RUCHIKA (TEXT):
Yes...story of our lives, Agastya.

Agastya chuckles softly, enjoying the banter.

RUCHIKA (TEXT):
Hey, need to sign off now. I'll talk to you tomorrow. And let me know when we can meet. Chief gave you a task to complete I believe.

AGASTYA (TEXT):
He did. I'll meet you with the data soon enough!

RUCHIKA (TEXT):
Bye then... go back to your work... I won't hold you back anymore.

AGASTYA (TEXT):
I didn't complain.

RUCHIKA (TEXT):
Hey, did you just try to flirt?

Agastya's eyes widen, realizing he might have overstepped. He hesitates, fingers hovering over the phone's keyboard.

RUCHIKA (TEXT):
Get back to work now. We'll talk tomorrow. Good night.

AGASTYA (V.O.):

It'll be fun working with you, Ruchika.

He stretches, a contented smile on his face, and turns his attention back to his computer.

Act 7

INT. LUXURIOUS HOTEL ROOM - THE ORCHID - DAY

The room is bathed in soft, ambient light. The decor is plush, with a large bed taking center stage. A bottle of Merlot sits on a table next to a half-filled wine glass. The curtains are drawn, giving the room a sense of privacy and intimacy.

RUCHIKA, a stunning woman in her late twenties, dressed in a light summer dress that accentuates her figure, paces the room. Her face shows a mix of anticipation and impatience. She takes a sip from the wine glass, her eyes darting to the door every now and then.

FLASHBACK SEQUENCE BEGINS

INT. LUXURIOUS BEDROOM - NIGHT

Ruchika with a BUSINESS TYCOON, passionate and intense.

INT. PENTHOUSE SUITE - NIGHT

Ruchika in the midst of a wild party with an IPL CRICKET TEAM CAPTAIN and other players.

INT. FILM STAR'S LIVING ROOM - NIGHT

Ruchika and a FRIEND with an AGING BOLLYWOOD ACTOR, the atmosphere charged.

FLASHBACK SEQUENCE ENDS

A hesitant KNOCK interrupts her thoughts. She places the wine glass down and strides to the door, her gait slightly unsteady.

She opens the door to reveal AGASTYA, a young man in his late twenties, looking both nervous and excited. His eyes widen as they take in Ruchika's appearance.

AGASTYA:
"Ruchika?"

RUCHIKA (teasingly):
"Yes, that's me. Do you want to check my ID?"

AGASTYA (blushing):
"Oh, come on! Don't embarrass me."

RUCHIKA (playfully):
"Well, you know what, sweety? I'm 'bound by duty' to show you my ID."

She retrieves a badge from her purse, flashing it briefly in front of Agastya, who barely glances at it. She then wraps her arms around his neck, pulling him close.

RUCHIKA (whispering seductively):
"Now, show me if you are as good in real as you have been in your texts all these days."

The tension between them is palpable as they share a passionate kiss.

INT. LUXURIOUS HOTEL ROOM - THE ORCHID - DAY

The room is dimly lit, with the curtains drawn. The sound of rain pattering against the windows fills the room. AGASTYA and RUCHIKA are on the sofa, their bodies close. The empty wine glass and bottle sit on the table.

AGASTYA (nervously):
"I - I got the information your boss wanted me to..."

RUCHIKA (interrupting, seductively):
"Can we please not jump into business?"

She places a finger on his lips, silencing him. Their eyes lock, the tension palpable.

RUCHIKA (whispering):
"What has developed between you and me over the last few days is far more important to me right now than what 'the boss' wants us to do."

She leans closer, their lips inches apart. The two become lost in each other, the outside world forgotten.

DISSOLVE TO:

INT. LUXURIOUS HOTEL ROOM - THE ORCHID - LATER

The room is in disarray. Clothes are strewn about. RUCHIKA lies on the bed, the white sheet draped over her, her hair a mess. She watches AGASTYA as he dresses, a look of mild disappointment on her face.

AGASTYA (awkwardly):
"I've got to go back to work, honey."

He hands her a pen drive.

AGASTYA:
"This has everything you'll need. When are we meeting next?"

RUCHIKA (feigning enthusiasm):
"Whenever you find the time, sweetheart."

She leans in for a kiss.

RUCHIKA:
"I'm so happy we met!"

AGASTYA, clearly on cloud nine, exits the room. Once the door closes, RUCHIKA's facade drops. She quickly dials a number on her phone.

RUCHIKA (into the phone):
"I've got everything you wanted."

She ends the call, her face a mask of determination.

Act 8

INT. ASHWIN'S BATHROOM - MORNING

The sound of running water fills the room. Steam rises from the shower, and we see the silhouette of ASHWIN SAXENA, a well-built man in his late 30s, behind the frosted glass door.

NARRATOR (V.O.)
Ashwin Saxena, the Sales and Marketing Director at NexGen, is a man who's always on the move. Today, he's racing against time.

ASHWIN (thinking to himself, as he showers)
I need to be quick. Shave, dress, breakfast, and then off to the office by nine-thirty.

NARRATOR (V.O.)
Ashwin's charm, eloquence, and sharp dressing have always set him apart. But it's his knack for building business relationships that's truly his strength.

INT. ASHWIN'S BEDROOM - MORNING

The room is tastefully decorated. On the dresser, we see a framed picture of ASHWIN, VIKRAM, and a woman - MANVI. Another picture shows ASHWIN with a beautiful woman, ASHIYA, and a young girl, NUSRAT.

NARRATOR (V.O.)
Ashwin and Vikram, friends from their management school days, share a history. They both dated the same woman, Manvi, who

eventually became Vikram's wife. But fate had other plans for Ashwin.

FLASHBACK: INT. VIKRAM'S LIVING ROOM - NIGHT

A younger ASHWIN and ASHIYA, looking scared and tired, enter. VIKRAM and MANVI welcome them warmly.

NARRATOR (V.O.)
When Ashwin fell for Ashiya in Delhi, her family opposed. The two fled to Mumbai, seeking refuge with Vikram and Manvi. It was here that Ashwin's journey with NexGen began, thanks to Vikram's referral.

INT. ASHWIN'S BATHROOM - MORNING

Back in the present, ASHWIN is wrapping a towel around himself when he hears ASHIYA's voice.

ASHIYA (O.S.)
Ashwin, where are you?

ASHWIN
In the shower, honey!

ASHIYA's muffled voice is heard again, but ASHWIN can't make out the words due to the noise of the shower.

ASHWIN (shouting over the noise)
What is it, Ashiya?

ASHIYA (O.S.)

Can you drop Nusrat to school today?

ASHWIN (recalling)
I thought your appointment was later in the day. What changed?

NARRATOR (V.O.)
As Ashwin prepares for his day, he's unaware of the challenges that lie ahead. The decision from Evita on the partnership proposal is due, and Ashwin's ambitions and past successes will be put to the test.

INT. ASHWIN'S BATHROOM - MORNING

Close-up of ASHWIN's face, lathered with shaving cream. He's meticulously shaving, lost in thought. The clock on the bathroom sink reads seven-forty.

ASHWIN (O.S.)
Sorry, I can't today, Ashiya. Why, I thought you said you were going to drop her to school?

INT. ASHWIN'S BEDROOM - MORNING

ASHIYA enters, holding a bowl of cereals. NUSRAT, their young daughter, is dressed for school, playing nearby. ASHWIN, now dressed, admires ASHIYA's natural beauty.

ASHIYA
The clinic rescheduled my appointment. I'll be cutting it close if I drop her off.

ASHWIN (rushing)

I can't today, Ashiya. I need to be at work early.

ASHIYA (pleadingly)
Please, Ashwin?

ASHWIN
I'm sorry, not today. I have to be at work by nine-thirty.

ASHIYA (sighing)
Alright, I'll manage. I'll drop her off.

INT. ASHWIN'S KITCHEN - MORNING

ASHWIN quickly sips his coffee, grabbing a couple of oatmeal cookies. The sound of ASHIYA and NUSRAT getting ready is heard in the background.

ASHIYA (O.S.)
Okay Nusrat, let's go! Put your shoes on!

ASHWIN checks his watch. Seven-fifty. He's satisfied with the time.

ASHIYA (re-entering)
Sorry I was whiny. I'll manage. Big day today, right? Evita's announcement?

ASHWIN (tying his shoelaces)
Yes, they are.

ASHIYA (supportively)
You'll make it, Ashwin.

ASHWIN (dryly)

Does it matter? My success is taken for granted. It'll just be another win for Vikram.

ASHIYA (confused)
What do you mean?

ASHWIN (heading for the door)
NexGen expects my success. It'll only boost Vikram's reputation.

ASHIYA watches him leave, a worried expression on her face.

ASHIYA (whispering to herself)
Something's changed. Why is it that success no longer excites him as it used to?

NARRATOR (V.O.)
A big day for NexGen. A pivotal moment for Ashwin. But most importantly, a defining day for Vikram.

Act 9

INT. NEXGEN OFFICE - MORNING

The elevator doors open to reveal the modern, bustling office of NexGen. The camera follows ASHWIN as he steps out, his face tense. The office is on the twentieth floor, with large windows showcasing the city below.

INT. NEXGEN OFFICE - ASHWIN'S CABIN - MORNING

ASHWIN enters his cabin, a spacious room with a large desk and a view of the city. He's clearly agitated, muttering to himself about being late. He powers on his laptop, tapping his fingers impatiently as it boots up.

CLOSE-UP of ASHWIN's face, showing his anticipation.

CLOSE-UP of the laptop screen, showing a flood of unread emails. ASHWIN's eyes scan the list, stopping at an email from ADI JUNEJA, Alliance Director at Evita.

INSERT of the email content:

Dear Ashwin and Vikram,

We regret to inform you that Evita has decided to enter into a partnership with another qualified technology company. We appreciate your endeavour in putting together a proposal for our collaboration, and look forward to future opportunities of working together.

Warm regards,

Adi Juneja

ASHWIN leans back in his chair, his face a mix of shock and disappointment. He takes a deep breath, trying to process the news.

CLOSE-UP of ASHWIN's phone as it begins to ring. The caller ID shows "VIKRAM."

ASHWIN hesitates for a moment, then answers.

ASHWIN (voice strained)
Vikram...

NARRATOR (V.O.)
A setback for NexGen. A blow for Ashwin. But above all, a disaster for Vikram.

Act 10

INT. NEXGEN OFFICE - MORNING

The office is buzzing with activity. ASHWIN walks purposefully down the corridor, his face tense. As he walks, he can't help but glance at SONAL, a young, attractive woman working at her desk.

CLOSE-UP of SONAL, engrossed in her work, looking up as ASHWIN approaches.

SONAL (smiling)
Good morning, Ashwin.

ASHWIN (with a charming smile)
Morning, Sonal. Looking gorgeous, as always.

SONAL (blushing slightly)
Thanks. Early meeting with Vikram?

ASHWIN (sighing)
Yes.

SONAL (whispering, looking towards Vikram's office)
He seems upset this morning.

ASHWIN
Tell me about it. This isn't going to be easy.

SONAL (teasingly)
My wishes and prayers are with you.

ASHWIN (smiling)

I'll need all of it.

INT. NEXGEN OFFICE - VIKRAM'S CABIN - MORNING

The door swings open to reveal VIKRAM, pacing up and down, visibly agitated. ASHWIN enters, closing the door behind him.

VIKRAM (frustrated)
This doesn't make any goddamned sense, Ashwin! Do you realize what this means for us?

ASHWIN (sighing)
I don't get it myself, Vikram.

VIKRAM (thumping his desk)
None of us saw this coming! Who's the other "qualified technology company"?

ASHWIN (pausing)
It's Alpha, Vikram. They were in the final shortlist with us.

CLOSE-UP of VIKRAM's face, showing his shock and disappointment.

ASHWIN (continuing)
I've already spoken to some contacts at Evita. I'll fill you in on everything.

NARRATOR (V.O.)
In the high-stakes world of business, unexpected challenges arise. But for Ashwin and Vikram, this setback was more personal than professional.

INT. NEXGEN OFFICE - VIKRAM'S CABIN - MORNING

The room is filled with tension. ASHWIN stands across from VIKRAM, both men visibly agitated.

ASHWIN (urgently)
Vikram, my contacts at Evita said our proposal and Alpha's were almost identical. It's as if someone had read every word of ours.

VIKRAM (incredulously)
What are you suggesting? That someone from NexGen leaked our proposal?

ASHWIN (hesitatingly)
It's the only explanation that makes sense.

VIKRAM (angrily)
Are you out of your mind? The only people who saw that proposal were Dev, you, and me. We've never taken printouts, and our emails are secure. How could it get into Alpha's hands?

ASHWIN (defensively)
I don't know, Vikram. But the similarities can't be a coincidence.

CLOSE-UP of VIKRAM's face, showing his frustration and anger.

VIKRAM (shouting)
Then who else, Ashwin? Who else could've leaked it?

ASHWIN (resignedly)
I'll keep checking with Evita. I'll let you know if I find anything.

ASHWIN turns to leave, the tension palpable. VIKRAM watches him go, deep in thought.

CLOSE-UP of VIKRAM's face, lost in thought, trying to piece together the puzzle.

VIKRAM (whispering to himself)
This makes no sense.

NARRATOR (V.O.)
In the world of corporate espionage, trust is a luxury few can afford. Vikram must find answers before it's too late.

Act 11

INT. NEXGEN OFFICE - AGASTYA'S DESK - MORNING

AGASTYA sits at his desk, munching on a slice of pizza. His phone rings, displaying VIKRAM's name.

AGASTYA (into the phone)
Good morning, Sir.

VIKRAM (V.O.)
Busy?

AGASTYA
The usual routine, Sir. Nothing unusual.

VIKRAM (V.O.)
Can you come to my cabin?

AGASTYA hesitates, glancing at the last slice of pizza on his desk.

AGASTYA
Be there in a minute, Sir.

INT. NEXGEN OFFICE - VIKRAM'S CABIN - MORNING

VIKRAM sits at his desk, looking serious. AGASTYA enters, looking slightly nervous.

VIKRAM
Agastya, how secure is our company network?

AGASTYA (taken aback)

It's... quite secure, Sir.

VIKRAM (raising an eyebrow)
Quite?

AGASTYA (correcting himself)
Very secure, Sir.

AGASTYA goes on to explain the security measures in place. VIKRAM listens intently.

VIKRAM
Has there been a breach recently? And I want honesty.

AGASTYA
No, Sir. I would've informed you.

VIKRAM nods, seemingly satisfied.

VIKRAM
You may go now. Thanks.

As AGASTYA heads for the door, he pauses, turning back to VIKRAM.

AGASTYA
Sir, you know that we do monitor staff emails and website visits, right?

VIKRAM
Yes, but that's internal. No one outside should have access to company emails.

AGASTYA
Yes, Sir.

INT. NEXGEN OFFICE - CORRIDOR - MORNING

AGASTYA exits VIKRAM's cabin, deep in thought. He pulls out his phone and dials a number.

AGASTYA (whispering into the phone)
Ruchika, we need to talk.

NARRATOR (V.O.)
In the shadows of corporate walls, secrets and suspicions intertwine, leading to a web of deceit and intrigue.

Act 12

INT. ECSTASY BAR - NIGHT

The bar is dimly lit, with soft jazz music playing in the background. DEV sits at the bar, loosening his tie, looking exhausted. The BARTENDER pours him a Glenfiddich on the rocks.

DEV (sighing)
Long day...

As he takes a sip, his eyes drift to a boisterous group not far from him. He recognizes ARUN SUNDARAM, laughing and toasting with his team.

DEV (thinking to himself)
Of course, they're celebrating.

Their eyes meet. A tense, silent stare-off ensues. Memories flood back to Dev.

FLASHBACK: INT. ALPHA TECH OFFICE - DAY

A younger DEV and ARUN sit in a meeting room. ARUN, looking smug, dismisses DEV's ideas in front of their colleagues.

ARUN (condescendingly)
Dev, your ideas are impractical and immature. We need real solutions, not theories.

The room is filled with murmurs. DEV looks humiliated.

        BACK TO PRESENT: INT. ECSTASY BAR - NIGHT

DEV quickly finishes his drink, trying to avoid ARUN's gaze. But ARUN, with a smirk, raises his glass in a mock toast to DEV.

DEV (muttering to himself)
That smug bastard...

ARUN whispers something to his group, gets up, and starts walking towards DEV.

DEV (thinking)
Here we go...

INT. ECSTASY BAR - NIGHT

The bar is buzzing with patrons. DEV stands at the bar, trying to keep a low profile. ARUN, a few steps away, notices him and raises his voice, drawing attention.

ARUN (loudly, mockingly)
Hey! Look who's here! It's Dev! The God himself!

DEV (calmly, raising his glass)
Hello, Arun.

ARUN (with mock sympathy)
Not a great week for you, is it?

DEV (trying to be dismissive)

You win some, you lose some.

ARUN (laughing, spilling his drink)
When was the last time you won anything?

DEV (smiling, but with an edge)
I forgot to congratulate you on Evita. But at least I take pride in my honesty. I don't find it exciting to win deals on stolen business proposals.

ARUN (agitated, slamming his glass)
What gives you that idea?

DEV (smirking)
Common knowledge in my team.

ARUN (face red with anger)
By your 'team', you mean Vikram? Mr. Casanova? And talking of honesty doesn't sound great coming from someone who set up his own company with ideas he had stolen from Alpha!

DEV (stepping closer, voice low and intense)
Arun, you know as well as I do, that it was you who never let my ideas become Alpha's ideas. You had no value for them… and when I set up my own shop, those very same ideas took away a third of your customers!

The patrons of the bar have now formed a circle around them, watching the confrontation. DEV gently pushes ARUN aside, making his way to the exit.

ARUN (shouting after him)

Let's see how far your ideas take you! It's the beginning of your end, Dev! And your blind trust in your team is going to cost you dearly, my friend!

DEV pauses briefly at the door, a thoughtful expression on his face, before stepping out into the night.

Act 13

INT. POISON BAR - NIGHT

The club is alive with pulsating music, flashing lights, and a crowd of people dancing and enjoying themselves. The atmosphere is electric, filled with a blue haze.

ANGLE ON: A GIRL

Standing in a dimly lit corner, she's on the phone, her voice barely audible over the thumping music.

GIRL (whispering)
I got him... Vikram's right here.

She ends the call and starts making her way through the crowd, her eyes fixed on a target.

ANGLE ON: VIKRAM

Standing at the bar, he's trying to get the bartender's attention.

VIKRAM (shouting over the music)
A Macallan with three ice.

As he waits for his drink, the GIRL approaches, standing close enough for him to notice her. She's strikingly beautiful, with cascading hair, big dark eyes, and full lips. Her musky scent fills the air.

GIRL (flirtatiously)
Hey, I'm Kaamna. Are you alone?

VIKRAM (smiling)
I am.

KAAMNA (suggestively)
I'm looking for company myself. I won't refuse if you offer me a drink.

VIKRAM (grinning)
That was fast! So, what's your poison?

KAAMNA
Whatever you're having.

As they continue their conversation, there's a palpable chemistry between them. The touches become more frequent, the glances more lingering.

           CUT TO: DANCE FLOOR

The two are dancing closely, their bodies moving in sync with the music. KAAMNA's provocative moves are clearly affecting VIKRAM. The atmosphere is charged with tension and desire.

VIKRAM (shouting over the music, into her ear)
Want to go someplace quiet?

Act 14

INT. ELEVATOR - NIGHT

The elevator's soft light illuminates VIKRAM and KAAMNA, their bodies pressed close. Vikram's hands are all over her, their lips locked in a passionate kiss.

KAAMNA (whispering seductively)
Baby, I'm so hot for you.

The elevator "ding" signals their arrival. They break apart, their breathing heavy.

INT. VIKRAM'S PENTHOUSE - NIGHT

The room is dimly lit, creating an intimate atmosphere. VIKRAM struggles to unlock the door, his hands shaking with anticipation. Once inside, the two are immediately drawn to each other, their clothes rustling as they get closer.

KAAMNA (breathlessly)
Give me a minute, sweetheart. I need to go to the loo… too many drinks.

VIKRAM (with a teasing smile)
Don't keep me waiting too long.

She heads to the washroom, leaving VIKRAM to undress further.

INT. VIKRAM'S PENTHOUSE - WASHROOM - NIGHT

KAAMNA quickly positions a hidden camera behind the slightly ajar door of a toilet-cabinet, ensuring it has a clear view of the couch in the living area.

   INT. VIKRAM'S PENTHOUSE - LIVING AREA - NIGHT

As KAAMNA emerges, VIKRAM, now shirtless, pulls her towards the couch. Their passion is palpable, their movements urgent.

   TIME LAPSE

   INT. VIKRAM'S PENTHOUSE - LIVING AREA - NIGHT

VIKRAM is asleep on the couch, exhausted. KAAMNA, looking composed, sneaks back into the washroom.

   INT. VIKRAM'S PENTHOUSE - WASHROOM - NIGHT

She retrieves the hidden camera, transferring it to her clutch.

   INT. ELEVATOR - NIGHT

KAAMNA, looking triumphant, dials a number on her phone.

KAAMNA (whispering)
We made it! You'd love the show.

The line goes dead. KAAMNA exits the elevator, stepping into the night.

Act 15

        INT. VIKRAM'S HOUSE - LIVING AREA - NIGHT

The house is dimly lit and quiet. VIKRAM enters, looking weary. He glances towards AYUSH's room, the door slightly ajar, revealing the sleeping child.

        INT. VIKRAM'S HOUSE - BEDROOM - NIGHT

MANVI sits up in bed, engrossed in a book. She looks up as VIKRAM enters, placing the book aside and getting up to greet him.

MANVI (with concern)
You've been working too hard, Vikram. You need to slow down.

She moves closer, attempting to kiss him. VIKRAM tenses up, turning his face away slightly.

MANVI (noticing his discomfort)
You've been drinking. Have you had anything to eat?

VIKRAM (avoiding eye contact)
Yes, I had. We dropped by a bar for a couple of drinks after work.

MANVI (probing)
Problems at work? You don't sound too… cheerful.

VIKRAM (sighing)
Yes. I had a long day; lots of meetings. Ashwin had to stay back as well. And more meetings in the morning tomorrow.

He begins to undress, clearly wanting to end the conversation.

VIKRAM
I'll take a shower.

MANVI (picking up her book again)
Okay.

As VIKRAM heads to the bathroom, MANVI suddenly remembers something.

MANVI
Hey, weren't you going to know if you won the Evita partnership today?

VIKRAM (pausing)
We didn't win. Evita decided to go with Alpha.

MANVI (surprised)
Really?

VIKRAM (sounding defeated)
You heard me.

MANVI
Damn! I'm sure no one saw that coming!

VIKRAM
You're right. That's the last thing we expected.

MANVI (curious)
Ashwin was on it, right?

VIKRAM (nodding)
Yes, he was.

MANVI
So, that was what all these late meetings were about?

VIKRAM
Yes.

MANVI (sympathetically)
You must be so pissed!

VIKRAM doesn't respond and heads into the bathroom.

INT. VIKRAM'S BATHROOM - NIGHT

The bathroom is modern with a large mirror. Vikram stands under the shower, letting the water cascade over him. He looks troubled, lost in thought.

INT. VIKRAM'S BEDROOM - NIGHT

Vikram returns to the bedroom, drying his hair with a towel. He plugs his phone into a charger and gets into bed. Manvi snuggles up to him.

MANVI
(Seductively)

"Come on! You can't be that tired."

VIKRAM
(Annoyed)
"Manvi, not tonight. I'm really tired."

MANVI
(Teasingly)
"Not even a quickie?"

VIKRAM
(With frustration)
"Manvi, damn it! I'm just not in the mood!"

MANVI
(Moving away from VIKRAM grudgingly)
"We hardly make love anymore, in any case!"

VIKRAM
(Blamingly)
"That's because you're always working late into the night on the accounts of your boutique… or, checking out designs in those stupid fashion magazines."

MANVI
(Angrily)
"I'm not 'always working late'!"

VIKRAM
(Shouting)
"It's four or five nights every week!"

MANVI
(Tearfully)
"This is not what I call being supportive, Vikram! You're never home. You hardly spend

time with Ayush. I'm the one who really has two jobs, Vikram; one at home and one outside. You do exactly as you want, just like every other goddamned man in this world!"

VIKRAM
(Shouting back)
"Manvi, I'm too tired for this right now! You are being very difficult!"

Manvi, frustrated, switches on the bedside lamp, illuminating the room and the tension between them.

INT. VIKRAM'S BEDROOM - NIGHT

The room is still dimly lit by the bedside lamp. Manvi sits up, her face flushed with anger. Vikram stands at the foot of the bed, his face contorted with rage.

MANVI
(With sarcasm)
"Oh sure, this is all my fault now! I am being difficult!"

VIKRAM
(Shouting)
"There you go! Now you will play the victim card. You are an oppressed woman now. A woman who's not being treated fairly!"

MANVI
(Angrily)
"Oh yes! Of course, I am oppressed! And exploited. And you bloody well know that!"

VIKRAM
(With disbelief)
"Really? What the fuck makes you oppressed? Do you ever have to wash a bundle of clothes? Do you ever have to cook a meal? Do you ever have to sweep the floors? There are maids doing all that stuff for you! There's a driver taking Ayush to school and picking him up. There are tutors to teach him. There's someone being paid to do every damn thing in this house! That does make you an oppressed woman, indeed!"

MANVI
(With tears)
"I can't believe this! I never thought you'd stoop so low! You know what, Vikram? It's your male ego... your weak, fragile male ego that's speaking right now."

VIKRAM
(Shouting)
"Really? You tell me I'm the one with a fragile ego? Your ego is so fucking fragile that you cannot handle a simple rejection for sex from a tired husband, without picking a fucking fight in the middle of the fucking night about goddamned gender issues! And I'm telling you this for the last time, Manvi. Stop acting like a victim, for God's sake! You know very well the situation we landed in last year, thanks to your feeling 'oppressed' and 'ignored'!"

MANVI
(Choking on her words)

"I'm shocked that you brought it up! I thought we had both decided that we'd put that incident behind us and move on. I'm not trying to defend myself. But you know very well that, it wasn't entirely my mistake. I had my reasons. I hope you remember the situation at that time"

VIKRAM
(With a sneer)
"Oh yes! The 'situation' - it was all my fault, wasn't it? Fuck you!"

Vikram moves to leave the room.

MANVI
(Shouting after him)
"You started this, Vikram. Now don't play the martyr by sleeping on the couch!"

VIKRAM
(Angrily)
"I didn't start. I am in no mood to fight with you tonight, Manvi. I am exhausted, for God's sake."

MANVI
"Yes, you did start, Vikram. You were the one who started with my 'always working late'!"

VIKRAM
"And you were complaining about no sex."

Vikram, furious, storms out of the room.

MANVI
(Shouting after him)
"Leave! Walk away! That's all that you're good at, Vikram Oberoi! You know what, Vikram? It's not your male ego. I was wrong. Ego has got nothing to do with gender. It comes from power. It's about authority. You have a God complex. It comes from your position at work. But, this is not your office, Vikram. This is home. This is family. I'm your wife. And it's not always about winning."

Manvi pauses, taking a deep breath.

MANVI
(Whispering)
"I sometimes wonder what'd happen if you were to lose everything one fine morning, your empire crumbling to pieces around you! Maybe you would turn into a better human being if your power were to abandon you. Maybe that would save my family. I so badly want to see you fall…"

The sound of a door slamming echoes through the house as Vikram leaves. Manvi is left alone in the room, tears streaming down her face.

Act 16

INT. VIKRAM'S CABIN - DAY

The room is bathed in the soft glow of ambient lighting. The walls are adorned with awards and framed pictures of Vikram with various business dignitaries. The large window behind Vikram's desk offers a view of the bustling Mumbai cityscape.

The door opens, and ASHOK PANDEY, a distinguished-looking man in his late fifties, steps in. He's dressed in a crisp suit, exuding an aura of authority and experience.

VIKRAM
(standing up, extending a hand)
"What's up, Vikram?"

ASHOK
(grinning, shaking Vikram's hand)
"I was with Dev. He is worried."

Vikram's smile fades slightly, sensing the gravity of the situation.

VIKRAM
(sitting back down, trying to maintain composure)
"Well… the last couple of quarters haven't been good."

ASHOK
(leaning forward, eyes piercing)

"To say the least. And I believe you were banking heavily on a partnership with Evita, which did not work out for us."

VIKRAM
(voice shaky)
"Yes. Evita took all of us by surprise, if you ask me."

ASHOK
(smiling wryly)
"You know what, Vikram? You allow yourself to be taken by surprise if you are not vigilant enough."

Vikram shifts uncomfortably in his chair, feeling cornered.

ASHOK
(leaning in closer)
"Dev and I have been discussing this for a while. We may have to make some decisions very soon about a restructuring."

VIKRAM
(voice rising with anxiety)
"What - what kind of restructuring?"

ASHOK
(leaning back, rubbing his hands)
"Well, it's too early to discuss this, Vikram. And I'll let Dev take his time to work out a plan. But we definitely need to be more proactive and more innovative. We need fresh ideas. And someone driven and motivated in charge of our business in India."

Vikram's face pales, realizing the implications of Ashok's words.

VIKRAM
(voice quivering, trying to force a smile)
"Looks like I might not have a job. So who do you have in mind, if I may ask?"

ASHOK
(laughing softly, waving his hand dismissively)
"Oh come on, Vikram! It's still you who's sitting on that chair! Everyone stays, including you. We would hate to lose someone like you. You've been with us for many years and we would want you to continue for many more. But, we have to start thinking out of the box, Vikram. Basically, pull up our socks, if you know what I mean."

Vikram nods slowly, processing Ashok's words, a mix of relief and apprehension evident on his face.

INT. VIKRAM'S CABIN - DAY

The room is still, the tension palpable. Ashok's words hang in the air as Vikram tries to process them.

ASHOK
"I have to tell you this. Ashwin met Dev the other day and presented a few ideas. He's a smart kid! Dev is mighty pleased with him. He thinks some of Ashwin's radical ideas may just bring us back in the game!"
VIKRAM

(forcing a smile, voice shaky)
"Ashwin?"

ASHOK
(nodding)
"Yes. Ashwin is a smart and successful guy, Vikram. The two of you go back several years. You know him better than any of us, don't you?"

Vikram's eyes dart around, his mind racing. He feels betrayed, cornered.

ASHOK
(standing up, extending his hand)
"Always a pleasure talking to you, Vikram. Don't worry! We'll tide over this crisis."

Vikram shakes Ashok's hand mechanically, his thoughts elsewhere.

INT. VIKRAM'S CABIN - DAY - LATER

The door closes behind Ashok. Vikram is left alone, the weight of the conversation pressing down on him. He paces the room, his footsteps echoing his mounting anxiety.

VIKRAM
(muttering to himself)
"Meeting Dev behind my back... Ashwin..."

He stops in front of his desk, staring at the Evita proposal. The betrayal stings, and he feels cornered.

VIKRAM

(voice rising with frustration)
"So Evita is now 'Vikram's idea gone wrong'..."

He clenches his fists, trying to control his anger.

VIKRAM
(whispering)
"I need to keep an eye on Ashwin."

His gaze drifts to a framed picture of him and Ashwin from their college days. The irony isn't lost on him.

VIKRAM
(voice filled with determination)
"There's only one person I can think of."

Act 17

INT. VIKRAM'S PENTHOUSE - EVENING

The room is dimly lit. Close-up on a whiskey glass. Vikram sits, his face tense, glancing at his watch. Cigarette smoke curls up from the ashtray, filled with stubs.

VIKRAM
(muttering to himself)
"I'd be damned if the bugger is on time even for once."

He reaches for his phone, about to make a call, when a soft, cautious knock interrupts him. He rises, moving to the door.

VIKRAM
(whispering)
"Finally."

He opens the door to reveal ALBERT PINTO, a tall, imposing figure with a peculiar appearance. Albert quickly steps in, looking over his shoulder as if expecting someone to be following him. Vikram switches his phone off as Albert comically pulls the blinds down on the windows and disconnects the desk phone, finally taking a seat.

VIKRAM
(raising an eyebrow)
"You look happy."

ALBERT
(whistling)

"I'm in love!"

VIKRAM
(teasingly)
"Really? Who's the lucky woman?"

ALBERT
(laughing)
"She was a client, actually."

VIKRAM
(sarcastically)
"I thought you had a strict 'never-fuck-the-client' policy!"

ALBERT
(winking)
"Well, you do make exceptions for seriously hot clients. I'm only human, Vikram! She hired me to keep an eye on her husband… he was away from home most of the time on business tours… turned out he was screwing his secretary… they were spending nights in hotels all over the city! I went to meet my client with pictures… that's a Friday… the husband was away, as usual. My client broke down. I tried to console her. Any gentleman in my place would. Wouldn't you, Vikram?"

Vikram remains silent, lost in thought.

VIKRAM
(whispering)
"Sounds familiar."

Albert chuckles, leaning back in his chair.

ALBERT
"Life is full of coincidences, my friend."

The two men share a moment of silence, the weight of their shared secrets hanging in the air.

INT. VIKRAM'S PENTHOUSE - NIGHT

The room is dimly lit, with the remnants of Vikram's whiskey still on the table. Albert sits comfortably, a file in his hand, while Vikram listens intently.

ALBERT
(smiling, reminiscing)
"I fixed her a couple of drinks to calm her down. One thing led to another. And we ended up spending the weekend together, barely getting out of bed… there hasn't been a single day since then when we haven't 'made love'…"

He makes quotation marks in the air with his fingers.

VIKRAM
(raising a hand)
"Enough, Albert. I get the picture."

Albert chuckles, pulling out a file from his briefcase.

ALBERT
"Your new recruit is clean."

He starts handing sheets over to Vikram.

ALBERT
(enumerating)
"Raghav Dutta, twenty-four… High school and university records… employment file from Tektronics. Credit card transactions, mobile phone bills, bank statements, travel records, call records..."

VIKRAM
(interrupting)
"How did you get all this? Some of this is confidential."

ALBERT
(smiling)
"You don't ask, and I don't tell. That's the rule."

VIKRAM
(sighing)
"I know, but..."

ALBERT
(interrupting)
"You wanted a check on this guy. He's clean. Anything else?"

VIKRAM
"No."

Albert stands up, heading for the window. He draws the blinds up, reconnects the desk phone, and Vikram switches his mobile phone on.

ALBERT
"I'll send you a bill."

He heads for the door.

VIKRAM
"Albert, wait. I have another job for you. Ashwin Saxena. Tail him. Round the clock. I want pictures."

Albert turns, his eyes meeting Vikram's.

ALBERT
(nods)
"Understood."

Act 18

INT. MAJESTIC AUDITORIUM - NIGHT

The auditorium is alive with energy. The deep bass of music reverberates through the space, and cones of light dance on the night sky outside. The audience is a mix of Mumbai's elite, with photographers and reporters buzzing around, capturing the glamour.

SUNANDA JAIN, Evita's CEO, stands on stage, her presence commanding attention. She finishes her welcome address and invites ARUN SUNDARAM on stage. The applause is brief.

ARUN
(smiling)
"Good evening, everyone. A lot of you must be wondering what brings the Head of a technology company to a fashion extravaganza like this. We'll not keep you guessing too long."

He gestures to Sunanda.

SUNANDA
(energetically)
"Ladies and Gentlemen, I'm so happy and proud to announce our partnership with Alpha Tech. The next generation of smart wearables and accessories, like this country has never seen before, will be part of our Winter Collection this year. Imagine an Evita overcoat that adjusts its warmth for you or

gives you directions with just a tap on the sleeve!"

The audience erupts in applause.

SUNANDA
(whispering to Arun as they walk off stage)
"We're using pre-recorded digital videos as backdrop for the ramp for the first time ever in Mumbai. It's going to be spectacular."

The front row is filled with celebrities. As the fashion show progresses, the audience is captivated, applauding each design that graces the ramp.

Suddenly, Arun's phone buzzes. He glances at the screen and smiles.

ARUN
(whispering to Sunanda)
"Excuse me, got to take this one."

He gracefully exits the auditorium.

    INT. QUIET HALL OUTSIDE AUDITORIUM - NIGHT

Arun steps into the quieter space, accepting the call.

ARUN
(smiling)
"Aarti Bansal! Always a pleasure to talk to you. I hope you don't have any more complaints about the money."

Act 19

INT. NEXGEN CONFERENCE ROOM - EVENING

The room is spacious and modern, with a panoramic view of Mumbai through the glass wall. The evening traffic below is a sea of lights, and the distant street lights along Marine Drive twinkle like stars. Inside, DEV and VIKRAM sit at the conference table, waiting.

The door opens slightly.

RAKESH BEHL
(peeking in)
"May I?"

DEV
(smiling warmly)
"Rakesh, come right in! We were worried you had left already. I have something very important to discuss with you."

Rakesh enters, taking a moment to admire the view before sitting next to Vikram.

RAKESH
(looking at the view)
"Beautiful, isn't it?"

DEV (turning his head perfunctorily)
"Yes, it is."
DEV (turning back towards RAKESH)

"But let's get down to business. You see, Vikram and I have been considering a merger with Quantum Technologies in Japan."

RAKESH
(raising an eyebrow)
"With Quantum in Japan?"

DEV
(reclining)
"Exactly. We need to expand globally, and instead of starting from scratch in a new country, partnering with an established local company is a quicker option. Plus, we can introduce Quantum's products to the Indian market as well."

RAKESH
(skeptical)
"It sounds like we stand to benefit more in this deal. Why would Quantum be interested?"

DEV
"They're struggling against giants like Alpha. We bring technical expertise, cash for scaling up, and a gateway to the Indian market."

RAKESH
(nodding)
"I see. So, what's the plan?"

DEV
(turning to Vikram)
"Vikram, why don't you take over? This project is your baby."

VIKRAM
(to Rakesh)
"The key is exchanging technical know-how and standardizing processes. We need to understand their operations and see if they meet our standards. If not, we need to determine the necessary investments to help them scale up."

INT. NEXGEN CONFERENCE ROOM - EVENING

The room remains as it was, with the Mumbai skyline outside. RAKESH, DEV, and VIKRAM are deep in conversation.

VIKRAM
"We just had a call with Quantum's CEO and their product engineering head. They're eager for a workshop with us on potential product collaborations. Plus, having someone in Tokyo gives us a chance to inspect their manufacturing plants firsthand."

RAKESH
"So, you want me to fly to Tokyo with our new designs and collaborate with Quantum?"

VIKRAM
(nods)
"That's right."

RAKESH
(raising an eyebrow)
"Isn't that risky? Exposing our designs so early?"

DEV

"We're drafting strict confidentiality terms. Quantum's security measures seem solid. We just need to ensure our designs remain protected."

RAKESH
(nods)
"I understand."

VIKRAM
"So, when can you leave for Tokyo?"

DEV
(looking weary)
"Rakesh, this might be our last chance to bounce back. It's crucial."

VIKRAM
(looking serious)
"I can't stress enough how vital this is for our future."

RAKESH
(smiling)
"I can leave as soon as the travel details are sorted."

VIKRAM
"I'll have Sonal handle the arrangements. Thank you, Rakesh. Good luck."

DEV
"Thank you, Rakesh. We're counting on you."

The three men stand, shaking hands in turn.

INT. NEXGEN OFFICE HALLWAY - EVENING

As RAKESH exits the conference room, he almost collides with AARTI, who seems a bit startled.

AARTI
(quickly)
"Hey, Rakesh. Vikram's still inside, right? He wanted this file before leaving."

RAKESH
(smiling)
"Yes, he's in there. I was just meeting with him."

Rakesh walks away, leaving Aarti looking slightly flustered.

Act 20

INT. VIKRAM'S BEDROOM - NIGHT

The room is dimly lit, with the soft glow of a bedside lamp. VIKRAM lies on the bed, staring at the ceiling, a trail of smoke rising from the cigarette in his hand. SONAL is beside him, covered by a white sheet, her gaze fixed on Vikram. The atmosphere is thick with post-intimacy tension.

SONAL
(softly, concerned)
"Is everything alright?"

VIKRAM
(taking a deep drag from his cigarette)
"I've always kept things to myself, Sonal. But I don't know why, for the first time in my life, I want to share my worries with someone. Things are not great at work, sweetheart."

SONAL
(sitting up, wrapping an arm around him)
"I've noticed. You've been different lately. More... on edge."

VIKRAM
(sighing)
"Work's been tough. We're not doing well, and Dev... he's not happy. I'm starting to question who I can trust."

SONAL

"Ashwin mentioned the Evita deal falling through."

VIKRAM
(nods)
"It did. And he's convinced someone inside betrayed us to Alpha."

SONAL
(choosing her words carefully)
"I've heard whispers... about Ashwin wanting your position when you got promoted."

VIKRAM
(smiling bitterly)
"I've heard those whispers too."

SONAL
"Do you think he might have sabotaged the deal to undermine you?"

VIKRAM
(clenching his jaw)
"If he's playing games, I'll find out."

A moment of silence ensues. Vikram takes a sip of wine from the glass on the bedside table.

VIKRAM
(smiling softly at Sonal)
"You know, it's nice talking to you like this."

SONAL
(smiling warmly)
"You can always talk to me, Vikram."

VIKRAM
(looking away)
"I rarely open up. With Manvi... it's different. We don't really connect."

SONAL
(raising an eyebrow)
"You've never mentioned her before."

VIKRAM
(nodding and whispering)
"There's this emptiness I feel. But with you, there's a sense of contentment."

SONAL
(teasingly)
"Should I take that as a compliment?"

VIKRAM
(laughing softly)
"You can."

SONAL
(pulling away slightly)
"Until the next attractive woman walks into your life."

VIKRAM
(pulling her close)
"That doesn't seem appealing anymore."

They share a moment of closeness, the world outside forgotten.

VIKRAM
(whispering)

"I've dreamt of a simple life with you, Sonal. A home, evenings filled with laughter, cooking together, and nights of passion."

SONAL
(smiling)
"That sounds unlike you."

VIKRAM
(smiling back)
"Maybe I've changed."

INT. MANVI'S STUDY - NIGHT

MANVI is engrossed in her work, the room illuminated by the soft glow of her laptop. The clock on the wall reads 8:00 PM. Her phone rings, breaking her concentration.

MANVI
(picking up the phone)
"Hello?"

MYSTERIOUS CALLER
"Is this Ms. Manvi Oberoi?"

MANVI
(confused)
"Yes, who is this?"

MYSTERIOUS CALLER
"That's not important. What you should know is where Mr. Vikram Oberoi is right now."

Act 21

INT. AIRPLANE CABIN - DAY

The airplane cabin is filled with passengers settling into their seats. RAKESH walks down the aisle, his face a mix of excitement and apprehension. He finds his seat and starts to settle down, lost in thought.

RAKESH (V.O.)
First time in Japan. I hope this trip is worth it. NexGen's future depends on it. I could also do with a change of scene after all these months of stressful divorce proceedings.

Suddenly, a sweet fragrance fills the air, distracting him. He looks up to see AMYRA, a stunning young woman in a hot-pink top and clingy jeans, struggling with her heavy bag.

AMYRA
(smiling)
"Hi, could you please help me with this bag?"

RAKESH
(stammering slightly)
"Of course."

He helps her stow the bag in the overhead compartment. As he does, she takes the seat next to him.

AMYRA
(smiling)

"Thank you so much. I'm Amyra."

RAKESH
(still a bit dazed)
"Rakesh."

They shake hands, and there's a lingering moment before Rakesh lets go.

AMYRA
"So, what brings you to Tokyo?"

RAKESH
"I work for NexGen. We're exploring a business partnership in Tokyo."

AMYRA
(excitedly)
"That's so cool! I work for a travel magazine. Tokyo's my next assignment."

The two continue chatting, getting to know each other better. The chemistry between them is palpable.

INT. AIRPLANE CABIN - NIGHT

The cabin lights dim. Passengers are settling down for the night. Amyra reclines her seat and curls up under her blanket. Rakesh, however, is restless. He tries to get comfortable, but it's clear he's distracted by Amyra's presence.

RAKESH (V.O.)
This is going to be a long flight.

Act 22

INT. COFFEE SHOP - EVENING

The coffee shop is softly lit, with a gentle hum of conversations in the background. SONAL sits at a table near the window, frequently checking her watch. The glass door swings open, and PRACHI hurries in, scanning the room until her eyes land on Sonal.

PRACHI
(out of breath)
"Sorry I'm late, Sonal. How long have you been waiting?"

SONAL
(smiling gently)
"About twenty minutes. It's okay."

PRACHI
(rolling her eyes)
"Yearly appraisals, bonuses, pay hikes... it's that crazy time of the year!"

They both chuckle.

PRACHI
(looking around)
"Did you order anything yet?"

SONAL
"No, I was waiting for you."

PRACHI
(signaling the waiter)

"I'm famished! I'll have a frappe with extra chocolate sauce and a brownie with ice cream."

SONAL
"Just a cappuccino for me, and two oatmeal cookies."

The waiter nods and departs.

PRACHI
(leaning forward)
"Sonal, I know this might seem sudden, but I wanted to talk outside the office. Just two friends catching up, okay?"

SONAL
(nervously)
"Alright."

PRACHI
(looking intently)
"So, tell me. What's happening between you and Vikram?"

Sonal's eyes widen, and she looks away, clearly caught off guard. She gazes out the window, where office workers are boarding buses, their day ending.

SONAL
(voice quivering)
"It's... complicated."

The waiter returns, placing their orders on the table, providing a brief respite from the intense conversation.

INT. COFFEE SHOP - EVENING

The atmosphere is tense. SONAL and PRACHI sit across from each other, their drinks in front of them. The hum of conversations continues in the background.

SONAL
(looking defensive)
"What have you heard, Prachi?"

PRACHI
(softly)
"I don't usually listen to gossip, Sonal. I wanted to hear it from you."

SONAL
(sighing)
"We... We're seeing each other."

PRACHI
(raising an eyebrow)
"So, the rumors are true."

SONAL
(nods)
"Yes."

PRACHI
(leaning in)
"How well do you know Vikram Oberoi?"

SONAL
(looking away)
"I... I know him well enough."

PRACHI
(voice rising)
"He's married, Sonal! Doesn't that bother you?"

SONAL
(voice firm)
"I'm aware. But what Vikram and I share is special."

PRACHI
(voice dripping with sarcasm)
"Special? Sonal, he was with Aarti not too long ago, and someone else before her. Look at Aarti now! She's shattered."

SONAL
(voice shaking)
"I've heard about Aarti. But Vikram and I are different."

PRACHI
(voice softening)
"Sonal, I've been around. I've seen men like Vikram. I don't want you to end up like Aarti."

SONAL
(teary-eyed)
"Prachi, I appreciate your concern. But I love him, and he loves me. That's all that matters to me. We'll make it work, no matter what."

PRACHI
(voice breaking)
"You're too young, Sonal. Too naive."

SONAL
(standing up)
"I don't care about his past or what the world thinks. All I know is that we love each other."

Sonal storms out of the coffee shop. Prachi watches her leave, shaking her head in disbelief.

Act 23

INT. HOTEL LOBBY - KINSHICHO, TOKYO - NIGHT

The hotel lobby is bustling with guests. RAKESH stands near the entrance, looking around, trying to decide where to eat. He glances at the list of restaurants and bars in the hotel.

INT. JAPANESE RESTAURANT - NIGHT

The restaurant is dimly lit and has a serene ambiance. Most tables are occupied by hotel guests. Rakesh finds a table and sits down. He orders a Japanese whiskey.

As he waits, AMYRA enters the restaurant. She's wearing a navy blue dress with white polka dots. Her hair is tied back, and her cheeks are flushed, indicating she's been out and about.

She spots Rakesh and approaches his table.

AMYRA
(smiling)
"May I?"

RAKESH
(grinning)
"Of course."

Amyra takes a seat opposite Rakesh. They chat and laugh, enjoying each other's company.

INT. RAKESH'S HOTEL ROOM - NIGHT

The room is dimly lit. Rakesh's laptop is open on the study desk, displaying product designs. The bed is neatly made.

The bathroom door opens, and Amyra steps out, looking refreshed. She hesitates for a moment, seeing Rakesh on the bed, holding up the covers invitingly.

She smiles and joins him. They share a passionate kiss, and she slips her hand under his tee.

The camera pans to the laptop, emphasizing its presence and the potential risk of the designs being exposed.

Act 24

INT. RAKESH'S HOTEL ROOM - MORNING

The room is dimly lit by the morning sun peeking through the curtains. RAKESH lies in bed, his arm around AMYRA. She's asleep, her back to him. He gently turns her around and they share a passionate kiss.

AMYRA
(whispering, teasingly)
"Hungry already?"

RAKESH
(whispering)
"Good morning."

They continue to embrace, but Amyra suddenly breaks free, leaving her dress behind on the floor. She dashes to the washroom. After a moment, she peeks out, beckoning Rakesh with a playful finger.

RAKESH
(smiling, to himself)
"What the hell! Looks like I'll have to skip breakfast!"

He jumps out of bed and heads to the washroom.

INT. RAKESH'S HOTEL ROOM - LATER

Amyra, now in a bathrobe, steps out of the washroom and approaches the desk where Rakesh's laptop sits. She notices it's off and quickly plugs in the charger. She boots it up, pulling out her phone to check a note.

AMYRA
(whispering to herself)
"Come on, come on..."

She logs in as an Administrator, using the password from her phone. She quickly searches the laptop, finding a folder named <TOKYO WORKSHOP>. She takes out a pen drive from her purse and begins copying the folder's contents, constantly glancing towards the washroom door.

Once the transfer is complete, she safely ejects the pen drive, shuts down the laptop, and unplugs the charger, leaving everything as it was.

Act 25

INT. TAXI - MORNING

Close-up on AMYRA's face, her eyes reflecting the Tokyo streets passing by. She's lost in thought.

The taxi halts. The Marriott Hotel sign is visible through the window.

INT. MARRIOTT HOTEL SUITE - MORNING

The door opens, revealing AMYRA. She's greeted by three JAPANESE MEN. The leader, an older man with a crew-cut, bows in greeting.

LEADER
You are five minutes late. We were wondering if you'd leave your lover's room at all.

The men chuckle. AMYRA, not amused, hands over the pen drive.

AMYRA
When I make a promise, I keep it. Here it is.

One of the younger men, YOUNG EXECUTIVE, takes the pen drive and plugs it into a laptop. The room is filled with tension. AMYRA glances at her watch, clearly impatient.

LEADER (smiling)
Please, have a seat.

AMYRA
Thanks, I'm fine.

After a few moments, the YOUNG EXECUTIVE nods at the leader.

YOUNG EXECUTIVE
Everything seems in order.

LEADER (turning towards AMYRA)
You've done well. Thank you.

EXT. MARRIOTT HOTEL - MORNING

AMYRA briskly walks out of the hotel, dialing a number on her phone.

AMYRA
The job's done. Everything's handed over.

A pause as she listens to the person on the other end.

AMYRA (grinning)
Are you sure I can't see him again? Just one last time?

Act 26

EXT. CHOWPATTY BEACH - EVENING

The sun is setting, casting a golden hue over the beach. Stalls selling chaats and pau-bhaji are bustling with activity. Couples and families are scattered around, some on straw mats, some walking along the shore. The Marine Drive is lit up, cars zooming past.

VIKRAM stands, looking around, checking his watch. It reads 6:55 PM. He's visibly anxious.

CUT TO:

ALBERT on the other side of the road, spotting Vikram. He waves and waits for the traffic to halt.

CUT BACK TO:

VIKRAM noticing Albert and nodding in acknowledgment.

CUT TO:

ALBERT crossing the road, looking a bit disheveled and tired.

ALBERT (sighing)
Good evening, Vikram.

VIKRAM
Good evening, Albert. Everything okay?

ALBERT (pointing to his chest)
I'm nursing a broken heart.

VIKRAM (raising an eyebrow)
What happened?

ALBERT
She went back to her husband. Our affair was a "mistake" she said.

VIKRAM
That's sad. Did she pay you?

ALBERT (grimacing)
She still owes me a few thousands.

VIKRAM
Never mind. You had a good time, right?

ALBERT (looking distant)
It wasn't just a fling, Vikram. I thought I had fallen in love. Finally...

VIKRAM
I understand. But let's talk business. Anything on Ashwin?

ALBERT (sighing)
Yes, let's talk business.

CUT TO:

Close-up of ALBERT's PHONE as he swipes through pictures of Ashwin in various settings - business meetings, dinners, and family outings.

ALBERT (voice-over)
Mostly business meetings... weekends with family... nothing suspicious.

    CUT BACK TO:

VIKRAM and ALBERT. Albert hesitates before showing the last few pictures.

ALBERT
And these... you probably know about these lunch meetings...

VIKRAM's face changes as he sees the pictures of Ashwin with Manvi. He takes the phone, swiping through them again, his face growing darker.

VIKRAM (whispering)
Ashwin, what are you up to? And what business does my wife have with you?

Act 27

INT. CITY BAR - NIGHT

The bar is dimly lit, with neon lights casting a soft glow. The atmosphere is lively, with the sound of clinking glasses, laughter, and music. The dance floor is packed with people dancing energetically.

AARTI BANSAL sits alone at the bar. Her face is flushed, her eyes slightly glazed. She's surrounded by empty whiskey glasses. She signals the bartender for another.

CUT TO:

Close-up of AARTI's face as she looks around, her vision blurry. The people around her seem distant, their voices muffled. Men approach her, trying to strike up a conversation, but she dismissively waves them away.

CUT TO:

AARTI's POV: The dance floor appears hazy, the music distant. She watches the couples dancing, especially the women, with a mix of envy and pity.

CUT BACK TO:

AARTI at the bar, her face reflecting her inner turmoil. She takes a large sip of her whiskey, her hand slightly trembling.

CUT TO:

AARTI making her way through the crowd, stumbling slightly. She pushes open a side door, leading to an open-air lounge.

EXT. OPEN-AIR LOUNGE - NIGHT

The lounge is quieter, with a few scattered patrons enjoying the night. The sky is clear, stars twinkling brightly.

AARTI slumps into a chair, her breathing heavy. She tilts her head back, staring at the stars. A tear rolls down her cheek.

CUT TO:

Close-up of AARTI's face, her expression a mix of anger, sadness, and determination.

AARTI (whispering, voice filled with emotion)
Vikram... I know you're falling... falling hard. You shouldn't have left me for her. I will finish you.

Act 28

INT. VIKRAM'S HOUSE - NIGHT

The house is dimly lit, creating an atmosphere of tension. The sound of footsteps can be heard as VIKRAM enters, clutching his phone tightly. He looks around, taking in the quietness of the house.

INT. VIKRAM'S BEDROOM - NIGHT

MANVI is busy at the cupboard, methodically removing clothes and placing them in neat piles on the bed. The room is filled with a palpable tension.

VIKRAM (entering the room):
What's going on?

MANVI (coldly, without looking up):
Nothing that would bother you.

VIKRAM (sarcastically):
Looks like you have your own ideas about what bothers me and what doesn't.

MANVI (turning to face him):
Learning from you, Vikram. Good that you're home on time, for a change. I've something to tell you. I've decided to--

VIKRAM (interrupting, voice rising):
Manvi, keep that attitude aside for a while, will you?

Close-up of VIKRAM's phone as he unlocks it and pulls up the pictures sent by Albert.

VIKRAM (holding the phone up to Manvi's face):
Care to tell me what these are about?

MANVI (calmly, looking at the sender's name):
"Albert"? Who's Albert?

VIKRAM (frustrated):
How does that matter? I've asked you a question and you better come clean!

MANVI (mockingly):
Come clean? Look who's talking!

VIKRAM (voice shaking with anger):
Manvi, I demand you to tell me what Ashwin and you have been up to behind my back.

MANVI (sarcastically):
Why do you ask, Vikram? Are you jealous? I thought you wouldn't care even if you saw me in bed with someone else!

VIKRAM (trying to control his anger):
Manvi, you need to know that Ashwin--

MANVI (interrupting):
What about him? Now he's the bad guy, is he?

VIKRAM (mumbling):
Let's just say that he's trying to act smart in the office. I cannot and need not tell you more than that. And now, when I see

these pictures, I wonder if the two of you together--

MANVI (smirking):
Vikram, tell me the truth, for a change!

VIKRAM (defensively):
What do you want to know?

MANVI (tauntingly):
You are afraid that Ashwin has let your secrets out, aren't you?

VIKRAM (swallowing hard):
What - what do you mean?

MANVI (smiling):
I'll come to that later, Vikram. Who's Albert?

VIKRAM remains silent, avoiding her gaze.

INT. VIKRAM'S BEDROOM - NIGHT

The room is filled with tension. VIKRAM stands near a chair, gripping its back for support. MANVI is visibly angry, her face flushed.

MANVI (accusingly):
Okay, let me guess. A fucking detective? You hired someone to keep an eye on me, you fucking asshole?

VIKRAM (defensively):
It's not how you think it is, Manvi-

MANVI (furious):
How dare you get someone to tail me, you dirty pig?

VIKRAM (stammering):
He wasn't tailing you. He was after Ashwin. And it's an office thing...

MANVI (sarcastically):
You haven't answered my question yet, Vikram.

VIKRAM (trying to regain control):
What do you want to know, Manvi?

MANVI (pausing):
This started a few days back. That night, I was getting ready to feed Ayush when I received a call. From a woman I did not know. She said that you were with another girl at that very moment—

VIKRAM (interrupting):
A woman? She called you up and spoke bullshit about me. And you didn't bother to find out who she was, or, even check with me?

MANVI (voice rising):
She called me every night after that first call, Vikram!

VIKRAM (incredulously):
What the hell! And you never bothered to check?

MANVI (screaming):

I did, you horny bastard! I did! But I didn't check with you. I called Ashwin instead.

VIKRAM (mockingly):
Ah, your ex-flame? Not 'ex' anymore, is he?

MANVI (furious):
Shut up, you filthy dog! Not every man is a lecher like you!

VIKRAM (raising his voice):
Here I am, holding evidence of you hanging out with an ex-lover behind my back, and you're the one who's shouting and calling me a lecher?

MANVI (voice shaking with rage):
Ashwin has told me everything!

VIKRAM (voice wavered):
What do you mean?

MANVI (screaming):
About your ways, Vikram. You're a fucking liar! You can look into someone's eyes and lie through your teeth without feeling anything!

VIKRAM (defensively):
Manvi, you don't have to trust everything Ashwin says!

MANVI (voice almost reduced to a hiss, grabbing Vikram's collars):
What should I not believe, Vikram? That you tell him to lie for you about late meetings

every time you come home late? That you've been using him as an alibi? That you carried on with Aarti for months? That there are these random hookers you pick up from bars? And now, there's a new girl in the office who's warming your bed! Sonal!

INT. VIKRAM'S BEDROOM - NIGHT

MANVI starts slapping VIKRAM repeatedly. He tries to shield himself, but the blows keep coming.
The room is filled with tension. VIKRAM stands near the bed, his face red from the slaps. MANVI is packing her clothes into a trolley bag, her face determined.

VIKRAM (muttering under his breath):
Ashwin, you bastard.

MANVI (furious):
Stop cursing him, Vikram! Doesn't suit you… doesn't suit you at all!

VIKRAM (raising his voice):
Manvi, this is all bullshit! Ashwin is trying to make me look bad. At work. At home. He's trying to fuck with my mind…

MANVI (raising a hand to stop him):
Don't you realize, you idiot, that I'm leaving you? And don't you dare try to stop me!

VIKRAM (in disbelief):
Manvi, what do you think you're doing?

MANVI (looking straight into his eyes):
I was going to tell you, in any case, about my lunch meetings with Ashwin and every single thing that I've come to know during those meetings.

Suddenly, MANVI's phone rings. She walks past VIKRAM to answer it. VIKRAM turns to see AYUSH standing at the bedroom door, looking confused and scared.

MANVI (on the phone):
Yes Dad, I'm ready. No. You don't have to come inside. Wait inside the car. I'll come down with Ayush in a minute…

Act 29

INT. VIKRAM'S PENTHOUSE BALCONY - NIGHT

The balcony overlooks the city, shimmering lights in the distance. The soft patter of rain can be heard. VIKRAM and SONAL are close, a cigarette glowing in Vikram's hand. The mood is intimate but tense.

VIKRAM (exhaling smoke):
I'm not going to go down on my knees and plead with Manvi to come back.

SONAL (searching his eyes):
Are you sure, Vikram?

VIKRAM:
I'm absolutely sure, Sonal. I was going to tell her about us, in any case.

SONAL (nestling closer):
What happens now, Vikram?

VIKRAM (kissing her forehead):
Don't you realize, stupid girl? Our time has finally come!

SONAL (playfully):
Are you sure about this? You are a free man now. And there's not going to be any dearth of women who would throw themselves at you!

VIKRAM (chuckling):
I've only two words for them - I'm taken!

SONAL (feigning surprise):
Oh, you are? And who's that lucky girl?

VIKRAM:
A certain Miss Verma!

They share a passionate kiss, the distant rumble of thunder accentuating the moment.

SONAL (pulling away slightly):
But how did Manvi find out about us?

VIKRAM:
Ashwin told her. They have been meeting behind my back. They used to be college sweethearts, you know.

SONAL (raising an eyebrow):
How do you know that Ashwin and Manvi have been meeting?

VIKRAM (smirking):
I have my sources.

SONAL:
And why do you think Ashwin would spill the beans?

VIKRAM (standing up, visibly agitated):
Don't you get it, Sonal? Ashwin is on a mission to destroy me! God! I need a drink!

SONAL (rushing to him, embracing him):
Calm down, Vikram. Just calm down, okay? You have me. We'll face this together.

VIKRAM (looking deep into Sonal's eyes):

I'm so tired, Sonal.

SONAL (softly):
I know, baby. Let's go to bed.

Act 30

INT. POISON BAR - NIGHT

The bar is bustling with the evening business crowd. The ambient noise of chatter, clinking glasses, and background music fills the air. The dim lighting casts a moody atmosphere.

Close-up: Vikram sits at the bar, lost in thought, nursing a drink. The weight of recent events evident on his face.

Suddenly, a hand lands on his shoulder. He looks up, startled.

Medium shot: Dev stands next to Vikram, a smile on his face. A few paces behind him, Ashwin stands, observing the interaction.

VIKRAM: (standing up, surprised) Dev?

DEV: (shaking hands with Vikram) Good to see you here. How are you coping with all this?

VIKRAM: (confused) All this?

DEV: (with a wry smile) I heard about Manvi and Ayush. Not to mention, the difficult times we're all going through at work.

VIKRAM: (guardedly) I'm okay.

Close-up: Vikram's eyes dart to Ashwin, suspicion evident.

DEV: Good for you. (pauses, placing a hand on Vikram's shoulder) There's a quiet booth in the corner over there. I've ordered a few drinks. We can talk for a while. Is that okay?

VIKRAM: (slightly apprehensive) That'd be fine.

Cut to: Ashwin, who smiles and raises a hand in greeting. Vikram nods in acknowledgment, not returning the smile.

CUT TO:

INT. POISON BAR - PRIVATE BOOTH - NIGHT

The booth is dimly lit, providing a sense of intimacy. Dev settles into a leather-padded chair, with Vikram and Ashwin taking their seats opposite him.

DEV: Well, Vikram. We go back a long way, you and I.

VIKRAM: (cautiously) Yes, Dev. We do, indeed.

DEV: And Ashwin and you have known each other for even longer. The two of you went to the same college, right?

ASHWIN: (winking at Vikram) We've been partners in a lot of unmentionable crimes.

Ashwin laughs out loud, joined by Dev. The atmosphere is tense, with Vikram clearly on edge, wondering what's coming next.

INT. POISON BAR - PRIVATE BOOTH - NIGHT

The atmosphere in the booth is tense. The dim lighting casts shadows on the faces of the three men. The ambient noise from the bar is muffled, making their conversation even more intense.

DEV: (winking at Ashwin) I'd rather not ask you about those.

Close-up: Vikram's face, clearly unamused by the jest.

DEV: (turning to Vikram, serious) So, Vikram, we're all friends here. Let's not beat about the bush. Let's talk like friends. I'm not going to bullshit you. And I promise, none of us is going to be judgemental.

VIKRAM: (impatiently) Dev, you said you were not going to beat about the bush...

DEV: And I won't. Look, Vikram. It's no secret that you enjoy the good life. But it becomes a concern for me if your... 'reckless' lifestyle starts affecting your performance at work.

Medium shot: Vikram, silent, his face a mask, waiting for Dev to continue.

DEV: And now I'm told that Manvi has left you. Your personal life is a mess. I'm not sure how that's going to impact your work.

VIKRAM: (agitated) Dev, who told you? How did you come to know about Manvi?

Close-up: Dev's face, showing a hint of irritation.

DEV: Why is that so important? We are all friends here.

VIKRAM: (firmly) That's important for me, Dev. I have every right to find out who's been talking about me behind my back.

Quick cut to: Ashwin, his face flushed, avoiding Vikram's gaze.

DEV: (ignoring Vikram's question) Vikram, I have a lot of respect for you. Your success is vital for this company. I want all of us to give our best at work.

VIKRAM: And what makes you think I'm not giving my best?

DEV: (voice rising) Results, Vikram, results. They don't seem to be speaking in your favour. And we all know why.

Close-up: Vikram's face, anger evident in his eyes.

INT. POISON BAR - PRIVATE BOOTH - NIGHT

The dim lighting of the booth casts a dramatic shadow on the three men. The ambient noise from the bar is muffled, but the tension is palpable.

VIKRAM (pulling out his phone, showing pictures): Dev, what you don't know is this.

Close-up: Pictures of Ashwin with Manvi on Vikram's phone.

VIKRAM: How do you think I'll be at peace when my friend is not only screwing me at work but also taking my wife out on secret lunch dates?

ASHWIN: (swallowing hard) Vikram, listen… I can explain this. Manvi was worried. She had been receiving mysterious calls from a woman. About you…

VIKRAM: And instead of asking me, she asked you?

ASHWIN: Yes, she did. She wasn't sure you'd be honest with her. Those calls were freaking her out!

VIKRAM: (shouting) Listen, Ashwin… Manvi tried to bullshit me with the same story. Save it for a fucking idiot, do you two get it? I'm not one!

ASHWIN: And who the hell took those pictures? Have you set a detective on me, Vikram? How dare you!

Medium shot: The two men are almost nose-to-nose, the tension palpable.

DEV: (interjecting) Boys! Look at me. Let's not digress here, okay? You two can fight this out on the street if you want to. But, I've no interest in who's dating whom, and who's getting prank calls on the phone! Am I clear?

Close-up: Vikram and Ashwin, both glaring at each other.

DEV: I'm talking to you, Vikram. I hope you will sort out your issues at home, stop living on the edge, stop dating girls from the office, and go back to doing great work. And I want the two of you to work together like civilized adults. We work together for the company, take it to new heights, and we make a lot of money. Isn't that what we all want?

VIKRAM: That's what we all want, indeed. Just that, things won't play out like the way you said just now, Dev.

DEV: Why not, Vikram?

VIKRAM (V.O.): Because Ashwin is a snake. Because Ashwin is eyeing my chair. Because Ashwin will do anything to get my job. Because Ashwin is probably fucking my wife, trying to mess up my home. Because Ashwin is a liar. Because I have no respect for Ashwin. Because Ashwin has no respect for me. Because you are ready to believe anything that Ashwin says. Because no one trusts me anymore.

VIKRAM: (voice breaking) Things have gone too far.

DEV: (leaning forward, whispering) They can be made to go back, Vikram.

VIKRAM: I don't think so.

DEV: (rising, voice rising) Listen, Vikram. I gave you this job. I believed in you. I gave you your start, I gave you all the help you needed, and I created opportunities for you. And I expect you to excel at what you do for NexGen, for me. By fixing whatever is wrong with your life. Do you get that?

Close-up: Vikram's face, a mix of anger and despair.

DEV: I've given my blood and sweat to NexGen and I'll not let you destroy my dream.

Medium shot: Dev storms out of the booth, pushing past Ashwin.

ASHWIN: (pausing, glaring at Vikram)

VIKRAM: (shouting after him) First Manvi and now Dev! Well done, Ashwin!

Act 31

Two weeks later

INT. VIKRAM'S BEDROOM - MORNING

The room is dimly lit by the morning sun. The annoying buzz of an alarm clock fills the room. Vikram's hand reaches out from under the sheets to shut it off. He groans, rubbing his eyes and trying to sit up.

VIKRAM: (mumbling to himself) Just a few more minutes...

His phone rings, breaking his drowsy state. He squints at the caller ID: "DEV."

VIKRAM: (answering, groggily) Hello?

DEV: (voice sharp and impatient) Where exactly are you?

VIKRAM: Getting ready, Dev. I'll be out in a couple of minutes.

DEV: Switch on the goddamned TV, Vikram! And head for whichever is your favourite business channel, unless you prefer watching porn over your breakfast!

Vikram's eyes widen, sensing the urgency and anger in Dev's voice.

INT. VIKRAM'S LIVING ROOM - MORNING

Vikram, in his pajamas, rushes into the living room, grabbing a glass of orange juice from the table. He quickly turns on the TV, flipping to Business 24X7.

Close-up: The TV screen shows a correspondent reporting from Tokyo. The headline reads: "Alpha Tech Announces New Range of Smartphones and Wearables."

The correspondent discusses the new features, and animations display the designs. They are identical to what NexGen had been working on.

VIKRAM: (whispering in disbelief) No... no, this can't be...

DEV: (voice from the phone, furious) This is on you, Vikram! And Rakesh! How did this happen? How did they get our designs?

VIKRAM: I... I don't know, Dev. I spoke with the team in Tokyo just yesterday. We aren't ready to hit the market yet...

DEV: If there's any foul play, Vikram, and if you or Rakesh are involved, there will be consequences!

Vikram's grip on the glass loosens, and it teeters on the edge of the table. He feels the weight of the world pressing down on him.

VIKRAM: (voice barely above a whisper) I need to figure this out, Dev.

DEV: You better. And fast.

The call ends. The room is silent except for the ongoing report on the TV. Vikram's face is pale, his world collapsing around him.

Act 32

INT. NEXGEN CONFERENCE ROOM - MORNING

The room is tense. A cold cup of coffee sits on the table. Dev sits at the head of the table, his eyes darting between Vikram and Rakesh. Rakesh looks disheveled, clearly unprepared for the meeting.

RAKESH: (nervously) There's no other way the designs could've reached Alpha! It must be Quantum. I've been apprehensive all along and...

Dev raises a hand, silencing Rakesh. He stands, pacing the room, deep in thought.

DEV: So, you're saying it's Quantum's fault? And we should investigate in Japan? Why would Quantum give our designs to their competitor, Alpha when they are collaborating with us?

VIKRAM: (defensively) Dev, I don't know how this happened. But I assure you, we'll get to the bottom of this.

DEV: (angrily) Vikram, first we lose the Evita deal to Alpha, and now this? It's too much of a coincidence. Your team, your responsibility!

RAKESH: We'll find evidence, Dev. Just give us some time.

DEV: One day. That's all you get. Or you're both out.

A knock interrupts the heated exchange. Nancy, the receptionist, peeks in.

NANCY: Sorry to interrupt, Sir. Mr. Oberoi, your wife is here. She says it's urgent.

VIKRAM: (confused) Manvi? Here?

NANCY: Yes, Sir. She insists on seeing you immediately.

VIKRAM: (to Dev) I'll be right back.

DEV rolls his eyes.

      INT. NEXGEN OFFICE CORRIDOR - MORNING

Vikram walks briskly, with Nancy trailing behind. He can feel the eyes of his colleagues on him. He glances at Nancy, searching for answers, but she avoids his gaze.

As he nears the reception, he catches a glimpse of a computer screen from a nearby cubicle. His heart drops.

Close-up: The screen displays a compromising video of Vikram with another woman on YouTube. Vikram looks around the office. All eyes are fixed on him.

VIKRAM: (whispering in horror) What the hell is this?

Nancy looks away, clearly embarrassed. Vikram's face turns pale, realizing the gravity of the situation.

Act 33

INT. NEXGEN OFFICE - MORNING

The office is buzzing with activity. Vikram, with a look of horror, approaches the computer screen where the video is playing. The employee at the cubicle tries to speak, but Vikram doesn't hear her.

Close-up: The video title reads: "NEXGEN BOSS CAUGHT ON CAMERA WITH PANTS DOWN - UNCUT VERSION."

VIKRAM: (whispering to himself) Kaamna...

Flashes of memories hit Vikram. The night at Poison, the penthouse, and the intoxication. He's in disbelief.

Suddenly, the office door slams open. Manvi storms in, her face red with anger. Without a word, she walks up to Vikram and delivers a powerful kick between his legs. The office gasps collectively.

VIKRAM: (groaning in pain) Manvi...

Manvi, without looking back, raises her middle finger at Vikram and walks out.

Dev approaches Vikram, his face a mix of anger and disappointment. He glances at the computer screen, then back at Vikram.

DEV: Disgusting! Leave my office, Vikram. And don't ever come back.

Vikram, still in pain, watches as Dev walks away.

Rakesh emerges from the conference room, having overheard the commotion. He spots the video playing on a nearby screen and recognizes Kaamna.

RAKESH: (thinking to himself) That's the same girl from Tokyo...

He's about to approach Dev but hesitates, realizing the implications of his own involvement with Kaamna.

RAKESH: (whispering to himself) I shouldn't say anything...

Rakesh retreats, deciding to keep his secret.

Act 34

INT. NEXGEN OFFICE - SYSTEMS AND NETWORK TEAM ROOM - DAY

The room buzzes with the hum of computers. AGASTYA, a focused young man, works diligently at his desk. The distant sounds of commotion from outside the room pique his interest.

AGASTYA: (to a TRAINEE nearby) Go see what that's about.

The TRAINEE nods, hurrying out. Moments later, he returns, eyes wide with excitement.

TRAINEE: Agastya, you've got to see this.

Before AGASTYA can respond, the TRAINEE quickly navigates to YouTube on Agastya's laptop. The video title reads: "NEXGEN BOSS CAUGHT ON CAMERA WITH PANTS DOWN - UNCUT VERSION."

AGASTYA's eyes widen in shock as he recognizes the girl in the video: RUCHIKA, with VIKRAM.

AGASTYA: (whispering, disbelief) Ruchika...

The rest of the TEAM gathers around, a mix of shock and amusement on their faces. AGASTYA's heart races, a mix of anger and betrayal.

AGASTYA: (voice shaking) Excuse me...

He pushes back from the desk, standing abruptly. He quickly pulls out his phone, dialing RUCHIKA's number with trembling fingers.

The phone rings, then an automated message: "The number you dialed is unavailable."

AGASTYA's face falls, a mix of hurt and confusion.

AGASTYA: (shouting to his team, trying to regain control) Back to work, all of you!

He exits the room, leaving behind a buzzing team and the still-playing video.

Act 35

INT. VIKRAM'S CAR - PARKING BASEMENT - DAY

The dimly lit basement is quiet, save for the hum of Vikram's car engine. Vikram sits in the driver's seat, replaying the video on his phone. The weight of the day's events is evident on his face. Suddenly, a knock on the window interrupts his thoughts. It's AGASTYA, looking anxious.

VIKRAM: (lowering the window, impatiently) What is it, Agastya?

AGASTYA: Sir, do you have a few minutes?

VIKRAM: I'm in a hurry. Anything urgent?

AGASTYA: I won't take long, but it's important.

Vikram hesitates for a moment, then unlocks the door.

VIKRAM: Get in.

Agastya quickly slides into the passenger seat. The tension in the car is palpable.

AGASTYA: It's about the video...

VIKRAM: (cutting him off, sharply) What about it?

AGASTYA: I... I know that girl.

VIKRAM: (incredulously) What do you mean you know her? She's a damn hooker!

AGASTYA: (taking a deep breath) Sir, I think we've been played.

VIKRAM: What's this 'we'?

AGASTYA: I've been conflicted about telling you... but I have to. That girl, her name is Ruchika.

VIKRAM: She told me her name was Kaamna! What... what's your point?

AGASTYA: She said she was part of an agency investigating a scam involving NexGen.

VIKRAM: (visibly angry) And you didn't think to tell me?

AGASTYA: They said it was covert. That I couldn't tell anyone, not even you.

VIKRAM: And you believed them? How could you be so naive?

Vikram thumps the steering wheel.

The two men stare at each other, the weight of the revelation hanging heavily between them.

INT. VIKRAM'S CAR - PARKING BASEMENT - DAY

The car's interior is dimly lit, the only sound being the hum of the air conditioner. Agastya's face is pale, sweat forming on his brow. Vikram's eyes are filled with rage and disbelief.

VIKRAM: (voice shaking with anger) You gave them my emails? For money?

AGASTYA: (voice trembling) They showed me IDs, they were paying well... I didn't have a reason to doubt them.

VIKRAM: (grabbing Agastya by the collar) You betrayed me! You betrayed the company!

AGASTYA: I'm sorry, Sir...

Vikram releases Agastya, taking a deep breath to calm himself.

VIKRAM: When did this start? Was it before the Evita deal?

AGASTYA: Yes, Sir. I believed them...

VIKRAM: (voice dripping with sarcasm) And you handed over confidential information to that... that woman? Ruchika? Kaamna?

AGASTYA: Yes, Sir.

VIKRAM: It wasn't just about the money, was it? She seduced you too?

Agastya looks down, ashamed.

VIKRAM: Answer me!

AGASTYA: (voice barely audible) Yes, Sir.

Vikram leans back, trying to process everything.

VIKRAM: So, someone pays you, gets a girl to manipulate both of us, and we lose the Evita deal. Then, they release that video, and I lose my job. Who is behind this?

AGASTYA: I don't know, Sir.

VIKRAM: When did you last hear from her?

AGASTYA: Over a month ago. She wanted Rakesh's laptop password. She said they suspected him of shady deals in Japan.

Vikram's face pales as he realizes the implications.

VIKRAM: (whispering) Oh my God...

He quickly grabs his phone, dialing Rakesh's number.

Act 36

INT. VIKRAM'S CAR - PARKING BASEMENT - DAY

The car's interior is dimly lit. Vikram's face is tense, his grip on the phone tight. Agastya sits nervously beside him, avoiding eye contact. The tension is palpable.

VIKRAM: (voice firm) Rakesh, I need you to be honest with me. Did you meet anyone in Tokyo? Someone who could've accessed your laptop?

RAKESH: (voice from the phone, defensively) What are you implying, Vikram?

VIKRAM: (voice rising) Just answer the damn question, Rakesh! Did you bring someone to your room?

Silence. The weight of the question hangs in the air.

RAKESH: (hesitating) Vikram, promise me you'll keep this to yourself.

VIKRAM: You have my word. Now tell me.

RAKESH: (voice breaking) I met a girl on the flight to Tokyo. We stayed at the same hotel, had dinner, drinks... and she spent the night in my room.

Agastya shifts uncomfortably in his seat, glancing at Vikram, whose face has turned a shade darker.

VIKRAM: (voice dripping with anger) And you didn't think this was important to mention earlier?

RAKESH: I didn't think... I mean, I didn't know she would...

VIKRAM: (interrupting) You didn't think she would what? Steal our designs? Sabotage our company?

RAKESH: I'm sorry, Vikram. I truly am.

VIKRAM: Sorry doesn't cut it, Rakesh. We're in deep shit because of your recklessness.

Agastya clears his throat, trying to diffuse the tension.

AGASTYA: Sir, we need to find out who this girl is. She's the key to all this.

VIKRAM: (nodding) You're right. Rakesh, I need every detail about her. We're going to get to the bottom of this.

RAKESH: She said she worked for a travel magazine and had an assignment in Tokyo... she left in the morning...

VIKRAM: And did you meet her after that morning?

RAKESH: No... Amyra said she would be out completing her assignment and flying back the same evening... even joked about the shoestring budgets that her magazine had... said she would have loved to spend more time with me...

VIKRAM: I hate to ask you this, but – but have you seen the goddamned video that has cost me my job?

RAKESH: Y-Yes, Vikram... I have. I know what you're going to ask next, Vikram. It was the same girl... the girl in the video is the one who was with me in Tokyo...Amyra...

VIKRAM (thumping the wheel again): Amyra! That's the third name I'm hearing!

RAKESH: What do you mean?

VIKRAM: The same girl used two other names on two different occasions and fooled Agastya and me! This is a conspiracy, Rakesh. They had access to passwords, emails, everything!

RAKESH: (voice from the phone, incredulously) But how? Only a few people in the company have access to those passwords!

AGASTYA: (interjecting) It's an inside job. Someone from NexGen is involved.

VIKRAM: Exactly. This isn't just about a girl seducing executives. This is a well-planned operation. They knew exactly what they were after.

RAKESH: But why? Why go to such lengths?

VIKRAM: Control, Rakesh. Information is power. They wanted to control NexGen, and they've succeeded.

RAKESH: What do we do now?

VIKRAM: We fight back. We find out who's behind this, and we expose them.

AGASTYA: And we need to secure our systems. Change all passwords, ensure no unauthorized access.

VIKRAM: Agastya's right. Rakesh, I need you to coordinate with the IT team. Make sure all our data is safe.

RAKESH: I'm on it, Vikram. And I'm truly sorry for my part in all this.

VIKRAM: We all got played, Rakesh. Now, it's time to turn the tables.

AGASTYA: We're with you, Vikram. We'll get to the bottom of this.

VIKRAM: Thanks, Agastya. Rakesh, keep me updated. We'll meet soon.

RAKESH: Will do. Take care, Vikram.

Vikram hangs up, takes a deep breath, and starts the car. The engine roars to life, echoing Vikram's newfound determination.

Act 37

INT. VIKRAM'S CAR - NIGHT

The city lights blur past as Vikram drives, his expression a mix of determination and frustration. The radio plays softly in the background, occasionally interrupted by news bulletins about the NexGen scandal.

RADIO ANNOUNCER: "...and in the latest update on the NexGen scandal, Vikram Oberoi remains unavailable for comments. The video has now garnered millions of views, and the public is demanding answers..."

Vikram turns off the radio, the silence in the car now deafening.

INT. PRESTIGE APARTMENTS - PENTHOUSE - NIGHT

The door to the penthouse swings open, revealing a dimly lit, luxurious space. Vikram steps in, locking the door behind him. He takes a moment, leaning against the door, trying to process everything.

He walks over to the bar, pouring himself a drink. The amber liquid glints in the dim light as he takes a sip, the burn a temporary distraction from his thoughts.

Suddenly, his landline rings, jolting him. He hesitates, then picks it up.

VIKRAM: Hello?

MYSTERIOUS VOICE: Mr. Oberoi, thought you could hide?

Vikram's grip tightens on the phone.

VIKRAM: Who is this?

MYSTERIOUS VOICE: Let's just say I'm someone who's been watching you closely. And I must say, your little video was quite entertaining.

VIKRAM: What do you want?

MYSTERIOUS VOICE: Oh, we'll get to that. But first, let's just say your troubles are only beginning.

The line goes dead. Vikram slams the phone down, his face pale.

He walks over to the large windows, looking out at the city below. The lights seem distant, just like his past life. He realizes that he's been dragged into a game, and he's not sure how to get out.

Act 38

INT. PENTHOUSE - NIGHT

The room is dimly lit, the only source of light being the television screen. Vikram sits on the edge of the couch, his drink on the table in front of him. The news anchor's voice echoes in the room. The word 'Recorded' flashes in the top-left corner of the television screen.

NEWS ANCHOR: "Ladies and gentlemen, we have with us tonight a brave woman who has come forward with some shocking allegations against the CEO of NexGen. Please note, her identity has been concealed for her safety."

A pixelated face appears on the screen. Vikram's heart races, disbelief evident in his eyes.

SONAL: "I never thought I'd have to come to this point. But the world needs to know the truth about Vikram Oberoi."

NEWS ANCHOR: "Can you tell us what happened?"

SONAL: "It started with subtle advances, comments about my appearance, inappropriate touches. I tried to ignore it, thinking it was harmless. But it escalated. One night, he cornered me in his office..."

Vikram's face contorts with a mix of anger and disbelief. He clenches his fists, trying to control his emotions.

NEWS ANCHOR: "Why didn't you come forward earlier?"

SONAL: "I was scared. He's a powerful man. I thought no one would believe me. But after seeing that video, I realized I wasn't alone. I had to speak up."

NEWS ANCHOR: "What do you hope to achieve by coming forward?"

SONAL: "Justice. I want him to pay for what he did to me and to others."

The interview continues, but Vikram is no longer listening. He feels like the walls are closing in on him. He grabs his phone and dials a number.

VIKRAM (frantically): "Rakesh? I need you to turn on the news. Sonal is on, I can never go wrong with that voice. She is accusing me of harassment. We need to act fast."

RAKESH (voice on the phone): "Vikram, calm down. I'll handle this. We'll get to the bottom of it."

Vikram hangs up, his mind racing. He feels trapped, cornered. The weight of the allegations, the video, and now Sonal's accusations are too much to bear.

He takes a deep breath, trying to calm himself. He knows he needs to fight back, to clear his name. But the odds seem insurmountable.

Act 39

INT. VIKRAM'S PENTHOUSE - NIGHT

The room is dimly lit, with the glow from the television casting a pale light. The whiskey glass is empty. Vikram is slouched on the couch, his face a canvas of confusion, anger, and realization.

CLOSE UP on the TV screen, showing Sonal's pixelated face as she speaks.

SONAL (V.O.)
"For months, Vikram Oberoi exploited me with promises of promotion and higher salary..."

VIKRAM
(murmuring to himself, eyes fixed on the TV)
Lies... all lies...

SONAL (V.O.)
"...I started believing him. I thought we had a future together, after all. I even thought of deleting the videos I had made out of desperation..."

VIKRAM
(shouting at the TV)
What videos? What are you talking about?

SONAL (V.O.)
"...But then, the video surfaced on the Internet today. You know, that was my birthday! How could a man in love with a woman have sex with someone else on her birthday? That broke me completely. It

flipped a switch inside. I told myself, 'This is it! I cannot let this monster of a man get away with this!' That's when I decided to come out with my story..."

VIKRAM
(thinking aloud, frustrated)
That damned video...

He reaches for his mobile phone and watches the video again. He watches intently, searching for any hint or clue about the date. There is no mention of the date when the video had been shot.

VIKRAM
(voice rising with realization)
How does she know it was her birthday?

CLOSE UP on Vikram's face, beads of sweat forming on his forehead.

Act 40

INT. VIKRAM'S PENTHOUSE - NIGHT

The room is dimly lit, with the faint glow of the city outside casting a pale light through the window. Vikram is sprawled on the couch, a half-empty bottle of whiskey on the coffee table. His eyes are glazed, but there's a sharpness to them, a mind that's racing despite the alcohol.

CLOSE UP on Vikram's face, deep in thought.

VIKRAM
(whispering to himself, connecting the dots)
There can be only one answer. It was Sonal who had set the hooker on me that night. It was Sonal all along…

FLASHBACK SEQUENCE:

INT. NEXGEN OFFICE - DAY
Sonal making lunch and dinner reservations for meetings with Evita executives, overhearing conversations about the Evita deal.

INT. NEXGEN OFFICE - DAY
Sonal making travel arrangements for Rakesh, chatting with him, finding out the reason behind his Tokyo trip.

INT. COFFEE SHOP - EVENING
Sonal talking to the same girl who seduced Vikram, handing her a photo of Rakesh.

BACK TO PRESENT

VIKRAM
(voice rising with realization)
She's been playing me... all this time!

He takes a long swig from the bottle, the burn of the alcohol doing little to numb the sting of betrayal.

VIKRAM
(voice breaking, almost tearful)
And I was ready to give up everything for her...

He recalls their intimate moments, the promises they made to each other, the future they had planned.

VIKRAM
(shouting, angry)
Why, Sonal? Why?

He throws the bottle against the wall, shattering it. He's breathing heavily, trying to control his emotions.

Act 41

INT. VIKRAM'S PENTHOUSE - NIGHT

The room is dimly lit, with the faint glow of the city outside casting a pale light through the window. Vikram is sprawled on the couch, a half-empty bottle of whiskey on the coffee table. The television is on, playing a news segment with Sonal's interview.

CLOSE UP on Vikram's face, deep in thought.

RINGTONE breaks the silence. Vikram's phone lights up. Caller ID: Aarti.

VIKRAM
(hesitatingly)
Hello?

AARTI
(voice slurred, mocking)
Watching the news, are we? Serves you right, you sick son of a...

VIKRAM
(interrupting, desperate)
Aarti, we can fix this. I need you.

AARTI
(hysterical laughter)
Fix this? With you? I've got a new job at Alpha, Vikram. With Arun Sundaram. You can go to hell. Oh, one last thing… do tell your wife that she sounds lovely over the phone!

VIKRAM
(voice rising with realization)
You've been the one calling Manvi? How did you know about my whereabouts?

AARTI
(mockingly)
Albert Pinto. Remember him?

VIKRAM
(shouting)
You bitch!

AARTI
(laughing)
Goodbye, Vikram.

CLICK. The line goes dead.

CLOSE UP on Vikram's face, a mix of anger, betrayal, and realization.

BUZZ. Vikram's phone lights up again. A text message. From Sonal.

CLOSE UP on the phone screen. The message reads: "Remember Rishi Bhargav?"

VIKRAM
(whispering to himself, connecting the dots)
Rishi Bhargav...

FLASHBACK SEQUENCE:

INT. NEXGEN OFFICE - DAY

A younger Vikram having a heated argument with Rishi Bhargav.

BACK TO PRESENT

VIKRAM
(heavily drunk, voice breaking, almost tearful)
It's all connected... Rishi, Sonal, Kaamna...

Act 42
Sometime last year

INT. INORBIT MALL, MALAD - DAY

The mall is bustling with shoppers. The atmosphere is lively with the hum of conversations, the distant sound of children laughing, and the soft background music playing.

PAN SHOT of the mall, capturing the various stores and shoppers.

CUT TO Sonal, looking radiant, trying to walk gracefully in her new four-inch heels. She's visibly struggling but determined. Rishi walks beside her, occasionally glancing at her with a mix of amusement and concern.

SONAL
(whispering, slightly embarrassed)
Rishi, do you think I'm making a complete fool of myself?

RISHI
(smiling reassuringly)
No way, Soni! You look totally sexy.

SONAL
(giggling)
The last time I wore these, I twisted my ankle at a wedding. Just imagine, the baraat was coming in and I went...

Suddenly, Sonal drops to the ground, clutching her ankle in pain.

RISHI
(laughing)
I don't believe this, nautanki! Acting it out in the middle of the mall?

SONAL
(teary-eyed)
I'm not acting, duffer! I've actually twisted my ankle... again!

Rishi's face turns from amusement to concern. He quickly kneels beside her.

RISHI
Damn! Really? Can you get up?

SONAL
I can't, Rishi.

Rishi, without hesitation, gently scoops Sonal into his arms. Their eyes meet, and there's a moment of deep connection.

RISHI
Don't worry, Soni. I'll handle this.

Sonal looks at Rishi, her eyes filled with gratitude and something more.

CUT TO Rishi carrying Sonal through the mall. Shoppers turn to look, some with concern, others with curiosity.

CUT TO Rishi at a medical store, purchasing a crepe bandage.

EXT. INORBIT MALL STEPS - DAY

Rishi gently sets Sonal down on the steps outside the mall. He sits beside her, carefully wrapping the bandage around her injured ankle. Their closeness is palpable, and the chemistry between them is undeniable.

SONAL
(softly, looking into Rishi's eyes)
Thank you, Rishi.

RISHI
(smiling)
Always, Soni.

The two share a moment, hinting at the deep bond and budding romance between them.

INT. INORBIT MALL, MALAD - DAY

Rishi hands Sonal a bottle of water. She takes a sip, trying to calm herself.

RISHI
Wait here for me.

Rishi rushes back into the mall.

CUT TO Rishi at the Hush Puppies store, picking out a pair of flat slippers.

CUT BACK TO Rishi sliding the new slippers onto Sonal's feet.

RISHI
See if you can walk now.

Sonal tries to walk but winces in pain. Rishi immediately scoops her up in his arms.

SONAL
(whispering, smiling)
Thank you.

They exit the mall, with all eyes on them. Sonal rests her head on Rishi's chest, comforted by his presence.

INT. CAB - DAY

Sonal and Rishi sit close, her head on his shoulder, the wind playing with her hair. They enjoy the silent comfort of each other's company.

INT. D'SOUZA UNCLE'S COFFEE SHOP - EVENING

Sonal and Rishi sit at their usual corner table, laughing, talking, and enjoying their time together. D'Souza Uncle watches them fondly from the counter.

INT. SONAL'S BEDROOM - NIGHT

Sonal lies in bed, talking on the phone with Rishi. They laugh, share stories, and eventually fall asleep with the phone still connected.

INT. COLLEGE CAMPUS - DAY

Sonal looks around, her eyes searching for Rishi. She spots him talking to another girl and feels a pang of jealousy. She texts him, and he immediately responds with a heart emoji.

INT. MOVIE THEATER - NIGHT

The lights dim, and the movie begins. Sonal snuggles closer to Rishi, who wraps an arm around her. They share a tender moment, their eyes meeting in the dim light.

As a familiar song plays in the background, they lean in and share a passionate kiss. The world around them fades as they get lost in the moment.

SONAL (V.O.)
I never knew a kiss could feel like this. I feel complete, content. I want this forever.

Act 43

INT. D'SOUZA UNCLE'S COFFEE SHOP - DAY

Sonal sits alone at the corner table, glancing at her watch. She's aware of a group of boys a few tables away, whispering and stealing glances at her.

Suddenly, Rishi bursts into the coffee shop, waving excitedly at Sonal. He makes a 'V' sign with his fingers.

D'SOUZA UNCLE
(smiling)
What is this, Rishi? You should never keep a lady waiting for so long!

RISHI
(cheerfully)
D'Souza Uncle, just keep watching! The lady will jump in joy when I give her the good news! A pizza for us. With extra cheese! We're having a party!

Rishi rushes over to Sonal, hugging her tightly.

SONAL
(laughing)
Phew, Rishi! What the hell is wrong with you?

RISHI
(flashing a paper)

Wrong? On the contrary, everything's beginning to fall in place, Miss Verma! Guess what this is?

SONAL
(teary-eyed)
Rishi, is it what I think it is? You - you've got a job?

RISHI
(jubilantly)
Yes, darling, your boyfriend now has a job! In NexGen!

The coffee shop patrons start clapping. Rishi stands on a chair, taking a dramatic bow. Sonal claps, her eyes filled with tears of joy.

D'SOUZA UNCLE
Today's lunch is on me, Rishi! God bless both of you.

Rishi hugs D'Souza Uncle, then turns back to Sonal.

RISHI
(serious)
Hey, listen… I've something for you here.

He pulls out an application form.

RISHI
They're looking for interns in their Finance and Administration departments. I picked up an application form for you.

SONAL
(teary-eyed)
You did?

RISHI
Fill it up tonight, and we'll drop it at their office tomorrow.

Sonal nods, lost in her dreams.

INT. SONAL'S BEDROOM - NIGHT

Sonal fills out the application form, looking hopeful.

EXT. NEXGEN OFFICE - DAY

Sonal and Rishi drop the application form at the NexGen office.

INT. SONAL'S BEDROOM - NIGHT

Sonal sits on her bed, looking at her phone, waiting for a call. She looks disappointed.

INT. RISHI'S APARTMENT - NIGHT

Rishi works late into the night, surrounded by papers and his laptop. He looks exhausted.

INT. D'SOUZA UNCLE'S COFFEE SHOP - DAY

Sonal sits alone, looking lost in thought. She misses the times she spent with Rishi.

NARRATOR (V.O.)
And then, everything changed.

Act 44

INT. OBEROIS' SUITE - MARRIOTT - DAY

The room is bathed in the soft glow of afternoon light. Shopping bags are scattered all over the king-size bed. Manvi stands in the middle of the room, dressed in a red off-shoulder fitted dress. There's a knock on the door.

MANVI
Come in.

The door opens to reveal Rishi, holding a couple of files. He looks around, expecting to see Vikram but finds only Manvi.

RISHI
(nervously)
Vikram Sir wanted these files before his meeting with the Press downstairs.

MANVI
(smiling)
Yes, Vikram called me a while back and said you'd be here.

Manvi moves gracefully across the room, picking up a robe.

MANVI
You may want to call him and check, Rishi. He wanted you to wait for him till he came back. He said he'd be back soon.

She gives Rishi a lingering look.

MANVI
Make yourself comfortable, Rishi. You may want to get something from the mini bar if you want.

RISHI
Thank you! I'd wait here, Ma'am.

Manvi steps into the washroom. Rishi takes a seat on the couch, trying to relax. He then notices that the washroom door isn't fully closed. A mirror on the opposite wall gives him a clear view of Manvi inside.

Rishi becomes tense, trying to look away but finding himself drawn back to the mirror. Manvi, seemingly unaware, lets her dress drop, revealing her black bra. She then turns slightly, her face hidden by her hair, and begins to unclasp her bra.

Act 45

INT. OBEROIS' SUITE - MARRIOTT - DAY

Manvi stands in the washroom, her heart racing. She's aware of the slightly open door and the mirror's reflection. She can see Rishi is excited. She hesitates for a moment, then continues to undress, her movements deliberate.

FLASHBACK:

INT. NEXGEN OFFICE - EVENING

Manvi walks through the office, looking around for Vikram. The office is almost empty, with only a few lights on. She approaches Vikram's cabin and notices the blinds drawn and the door closed. She hears muffled sounds coming from inside. Curiosity piqued, she leans in to listen.

MANVI
(whispering to herself)
What's going on?

She carefully peeks through a gap in the blinds. Her eyes widen in shock as she sees Vikram with a younger woman, presumably Aarti. The scene inside is intimate and compromising.

Manvi's face contorts with pain and betrayal. Tears form in her eyes. She stumbles back, trying to process what she's just seen.

MANVI
(whispering, choked up)
Vikram...

She turns and rushes out of the office, trying to hold back her tears. The security guard looks up in surprise as she hurries past him.

SECURITY GUARD
(confused)
Ma'am? Is everything okay?

Manvi doesn't respond. She pushes through the exit door, her heels clicking loudly against the floor.

END OF FLASHBACK

INT. OBEROIS' SUITE - MARRIOTT - DAY

Back in the suite, Manvi takes a deep breath, trying to shake off the painful memory. She finishes undressing and steps into the shower, letting the water wash over her.

INT. OBEROIS' SUITE - MARRIOTT - DAY

Manvi stands in front of the mirror, her reflection showing a woman battling with her insecurities. The memory of Rishi's reaction to her undressing brings a hint of a smile to her face. She feels a surge of confidence and desire.

MANVI
(whispering to herself)
Maybe I still have it...

She takes a deep breath and steps out of the washroom, her eyes locked onto Rishi. He stands up, looking flustered and unsure of what to do next. Manvi approaches him with a sultry confidence.

MANVI
(whispering)
Don't be shy...

She pulls him close, their lips inches apart. Just as they're about to kiss, the door clicks open. Vikram enters, his face showing shock and anger.

VIKRAM
(in disbelief)
What the hell is going on here?

Manvi pulls away, her face flushed with embarrassment. She rushes back inside the washroom, leaving Rishi and Vikram alone.

Vikram's anger boils over. He lunges at Rishi, throwing punches. Rishi tries to defend himself but is overwhelmed by Vikram's rage.

RISHI
(trying to speak)

Sir, I... I didn't...

VIKRAM
(shouting)
You dare you touch my wife?!

Manvi emerges from the washroom, her face a mix of fear and concern.

MANVI
(pleadingly)
Vikram, stop! It's not his fault!

Vikram pushes her away, his focus solely on Rishi. The room is filled with tension, anger, and regret.

Act 46

INT. OBEROIS' SUITE - MARRIOTT - DAY

The room is tense. Vikram stands near the window, his back to the room, speaking on the phone.

VIKRAM
(into the phone)
This is Vikram Oberoi. Send security to my suite immediately. There's been an intrusion.

Rishi sits on the couch, looking defeated. His face is bruised, his shirt untucked, and his spirit crushed. He avoids eye contact, staring at the carpet.

Vikram hangs up the phone and turns to face Rishi, his eyes filled with anger and contempt.

VIKRAM
(voice dripping with venom)
Listen carefully. You will never show your face around me or my family again. Understand?

Rishi nods weakly, still not meeting Vikram's eyes.

VIKRAM
And consider yourself lucky I'm not handing you over to the police.

There's a knock on the door. Vikram opens it to reveal two burly security guards. The senior guard looks at Rishi, then back at Vikram.

SENIOR GUARD
What seems to be the problem, Sir?

VIKRAM
(pointing at Rishi)
He misbehaved with my wife. I want him out of this hotel immediately.

SENIOR GUARD
(raising an eyebrow)
How did he get in here? Do you know him?

VIKRAM
Yes, he worked for me. I fired him this morning. He tricked his way in while I was out.

The senior guard looks at Rishi with a mix of pity and disdain.

SENIOR GUARD
(to his companion)
Just a kid. What's the world coming to?

Without warning, the senior guard smacks Rishi across the face. Rishi winces in pain, his eyes watering.

INT. OBEROIS' SUITE - MARRIOTT - DAY

The atmosphere is tense. The senior guard looks at Vikram, concern evident in his eyes.

SENIOR GUARD
Is Ma'am okay, Sir?

VIKRAM
She's in shock, but she's okay.

The door to the bedroom is slightly ajar, hinting at Manvi's presence inside.

SENIOR GUARD
We should hand him over to the police.

The guard's companion, eager to prove himself, slaps Rishi hard across the face.

VIKRAM
(trying to sound magnanimous)
He's just a kid, fresh out of college. A police complaint will ruin his life.

Vikram glances at his watch, growing impatient.

VIKRAM
Let's get him out of here. I have a meeting to attend.

INT. MARRIOTT LOBBY - DAY

The elevator doors open, revealing Vikram, Rishi, and the two guards. More security personnel approach, sensing the tension.

SECURITY GUARD
(to Vikram)
Everything okay, Sir?

SENIOR GUARD
(to his colleague)
He misbehaved with Sir's wife.

SECURITY GUARD
Should we call the police?

VIKRAM
(interrupting)
No one calls the police.

Press photographers and reporters, already in the lobby for the NexGen event, begin to gather around, sensing a story. The security personnel, enjoying the attention, start to embellish the story.

SENIOR GUARD
It was an attempted rape!

GUARD'S COMPANION
He was fired this morning and wanted revenge!

SENIOR GUARD
Sir is too kind to press charges.

Vikram, realizing the situation is spiraling out of control, decides to take charge.

VIKRAM
(to the reporters)

The press briefing will continue as planned. My personal issues won't interfere with my work. As for the boy, I believe in second chances. I won't press charges.

The reporters eat up Vikram's words, seeing him as a magnanimous figure. Two guards grab Rishi, dragging him towards the exit.

VIKRAM
(to himself)
This might just work in my favor.

The cameras turn to Rishi, painting him as the villain of the story. As the guards throw him out of the hotel, Rishi manages to hail a cab. Inside, he finally lets his tears flow.

Act 47

INT. SONAL'S DINING ROOM - NIGHT

The room is softly lit. A dining table is set for dinner. The TV plays in the background. Sonal sits at the table, lost in thought, occasionally glancing at her phone.

TV NEWSREADER (V.O.)
"In a shocking incident, an intern with NexGen, who had been expelled from the company earlier today, tried to molest the wife of a senior leader of the firm in an act of retaliation."

Sonal's eyes dart to the TV. The visuals show a crowded hotel lobby, press photographers, reporters, and security guards dragging a blurred figure.

SONAL'S FATHER
"NexGen… isn't that the company where Rishi works?"

SONAL
"Yes, Papa."

Sonal quickly grabs the remote and changes the channel. The same news is being aired. She recognizes Rishi's T-shirt and red stone bracelet.

```
SONAL'S MOTHER
"What's going on, Sonal?"

SONAL
"I... I need to make a call."
```

Act 48

INT. SONAL'S BEDROOM - NIGHT

Sonal sits on her bed, phone in hand. The room is dimly lit. She dials a number, waiting anxiously.

INT. BHARGAV LIVING ROOM - NIGHT

The room is dark, save for the faint glow of a switched-off TV. Anupama sits on the couch, visibly distressed. The phone rings, breaking the silence. She picks it up immediately.

RISHI'S MOTHER (V.O.)
"Hello?"

SONAL
"Aunty, it's Sonal."
ANUPAMA
"Hello, Sonal."

SONAL (V.O.)
"Aunty, is everything ok? I've been trying to reach Rishi all evening… and now, the news channels…"

Anupama's eyes well up with tears.

ANUPAMA
"Sonal, we've no idea what's going on!"

SONAL (V.O.)
"Aunty, is Rishi home? Why isn't he taking my calls? His phone is switched off."

ANUPAMA
"He came home early... he has bruises all over... said he had slipped and fallen... went straight to his room... said he was tired..."

SONAL (V.O.)
"Aunty, I'm coming over!"

ANUPAMA
"No use, Sonal... he's sleeping... he doesn't want to see anyone..."

Anupama breaks down, handing the phone to Manoj.

INT. SONAL'S BEDROOM - NIGHT

Sonal listens intently, her face a mix of worry and confusion.

MANOJ (V.O.)
"Hello, beta. Don't worry. Rishi is very upset. There must have been a terrible misunderstanding. These television channels... I'm sure it'll be fine tomorrow. Rishi will tell us everything. I'll ask him to call you. Or, better still, you can come over in the morning and we can have breakfast together."

SONAL
"Uncle, did Rishi leave any message for me?"

There's a pause.

MANOJ (V.O.)

"Go to sleep, it's too late right now, beta."

Sonal hangs up, her hands trembling. She looks lost.

Act 49

INT. SONAL'S BEDROOM - NIGHT

It's late in the night. The room is dark, save for the faint glow of a streetlight filtering through the curtains. Sonal's phone vibrates on her bedside table. She groggily reaches for it.

INT. BHARGAV LIVING ROOM - NIGHT

Manoj sits on the couch, his face pale and eyes red from crying. Anupama's wails echo in the background. He takes a deep breath and dials a number.

INT. SONAL'S BEDROOM - NIGHT

Sonal answers the call, her voice groggy.

SONAL
"Hello?"

MANOJ (V.O.)
(voice breaking) "Sonal... Rishi... he's gone."

Sonal's eyes widen in shock.

SONAL
"What do you mean, Uncle?"

MANOJ (V.O.)
"We found him... he hung himself."

Sonal's phone slips from her hand, crashing onto the floor. Her face contorts in pain, tears streaming down her face.

INT. SONAL'S LIVING ROOM - NIGHT

Sonal's parents rush into her room, alarmed by her cries. They hold her, trying to console her, but her grief is inconsolable.

INT. SONAL'S BEDROOM - MORNING

The room is bathed in soft morning light. Newspapers are scattered on the bed, each with Rishi's face on the front page. The headlines scream about the tragic incident.

INT. TV STUDIO - DAY

A news anchor sits behind a desk, papers in hand.

ANCHOR
"In a shocking turn of events, the young intern involved in the NexGen scandal was found dead in his room last night."

The screen splits, showing clips of Vikram Oberoi giving interviews.

VIKRAM OBEROI
"We had given him a second chance. It's tragic that he chose this path."

INT. SONAL'S LIVING ROOM - DAY

Sonal sits on the couch, numbly watching the news. The weight of the tragedy evident in her eyes.

Act 50

INT. RISHI'S BEDROOM - DAY

The room is filled with a somber atmosphere. Sunlight filters through the curtains, casting a soft glow on the room. Sonal steps in, her face pale and eyes red from crying. She looks around, taking in the familiar surroundings, now depressive under the weight of Rishi's absence.

CLOSE UP on the TV, the laptop, and the neatly arranged books.

SONAL
(whispering to herself) "You always loved order, didn't you?"

She walks over to the desk, her fingers brushing over the diary. She hesitates for a moment, then picks it up.

CLOSE UP on the diary's last entry. The date is clearly visible.

SONAL
(voice breaking) "Oh, Rishi..."

She sits on the edge of the bed, engrossed in reading, tears streaming down her face.

INT. RISHI'S BEDROOM - DAY

The sound of rain pelting against the window fills the room. Sonal is still seated on the bed, the diary clutched in her hands. Her face is a mix of grief, anger, and determination.

SONAL
(whispering to herself) "Vikram Oberoi... you will pay for this."

INT. NEXGEN OFFICE - DAY

Sonal walks into the bustling office, her face determined. She's dressed professionally, her posture confident.

CLOSE UP on a nameplate that reads: "Sonal Verma - Administration Intern."

SONAL
(voiceover) "This is just the beginning, Vikram. I'll bring you down to dust."

Act 51

INT. PUBLIC PHONE BOOTH - DAY

The booth is dimly lit, with a hint of sunlight filtering through the gaps. Sonal stands, phone in hand, looking anxious.

SONAL
(into the phone) "I would like to speak to Mr. Arun Sundaram."

    CUT TO: INT. ALPHA TECH RECEPTION - DAY

The receptionist sits behind a modern desk, surrounded by the company's branding.

RECEPTIONIST
(smiling) "Just a moment, please."

    CUT TO: INT. ARUN SUNDARAM'S OFFICE - DAY

Vaibhavi, a professional-looking secretary, picks up the phone.

VAIBHAVI
"Good Morning, this is Arun Sundaram's office. How can I help you?"

    CUT BACK TO: INT. PUBLIC PHONE BOOTH - DAY

Sonal takes a deep breath.

SONAL
"My name is Sonal Verma. I need to meet Mr. Sundaram. It's confidential."

CUT TO: INT. ARUN SUNDARAM'S OFFICE - DAY

Vaibhavi hesitates, glancing at Arun's closed office door.

VAIBHAVI
"I'm sorry, but I need to know the reason."

SONAL
(voiceover, as Vaibhavi listens) "Tell him I work for NexGen. This is important for me, and more for him."

Vaibhavi's eyes widen slightly.

CUT TO: INT. ARUN SUNDARAM'S PERSONAL OFFICE - DAY

Vaibhavi knocks and enters. Arun is engrossed in his work.

VAIBHAVI
"Sir, there's a Sonal Verma from NexGen on the phone. She insists it's urgent and the matter is of utmost importance to… you, Sir."

Arun looks up, intrigued.

ARUN
"From NexGen? Set up a meeting. Not here, at the Club. Tomorrow evening.

Act 52

INT. ARUN'S CLUB - NIGHT

The club is upscale, with a hint of old-world charm. Soft jazz music plays in the background. The distant sound of chatter and clinking glasses fills the air. The golf course is visible in the background, trees silhouetted against the night sky. The atmosphere is relaxed, but there's an underlying tension.

ARUN
(mid-40s, sharp suit, confident demeanor) sits at a table, sipping his beer. He looks up as SONAL (early 20s, dressed professionally but with an edge) approaches.

ARUN
(slightly surprised) "Sonal Verma, what brings you here?"

SONAL
(taking a deep breath, trying to maintain composure) "Mr. Sundaram, I have a proposition that will benefit both of us."

ARUN
(raising an eyebrow, intrigued) "Did you say 'us'? I don't think NexGen and Alpha can have any common interest whatsoever."

SONAL
(leaning in, voice firm) "I'm not representing NexGen's interest here. Let's just say that I have a more selfish agenda."

ARUN
(suspiciously, glancing around) "I hope this isn't one of Vikram's dirty tricks. I won't be surprised if I find out later that I was being filmed all this while."

SONAL
(intensely, eyes locked onto Arun's) "Mr. Sundaram, hear me out. You have nothing to lose. But, we have a lot to gain if we help each other."

ARUN
(signaling the waiter, trying to remain nonchalant) "So, what's your 'selfish agenda'?"

SONAL
(voice filled with bitterness) "There's nothing that would make me happier than to see Vikram Oberoi lick the dust."

ARUN
(laughing, trying to lighten the mood) "That certainly is a delightful thought. But how do you propose to make that happen?"

SONAL
(leaning in closer, voice low and urgent) "Just hear me out."

CUTAWAY SHOT to other club patrons, oblivious to the intense conversation happening between Sonal and Arun.

INT. ARUN'S CLUB - NIGHT

The club's ambiance is still relaxed, but the tension between Arun and Sonal is palpable. The distant sound of chatter and clinking glasses continues. The golf course remains visible in the background, trees silhouetted against the night sky.

SONAL
(resolute) "Mr. Sundaram, if there's anyone who can destroy NexGen, it's you. Especially if you have access to classified information. And some luck."

ARUN
(laughing, mocking) "So, the Admin interns at NexGen also do market research when they aren't making hotel and flight reservations?"

SONAL
(voice firm, eyes locked onto Arun's) "You tell me about those projects where you are competing with NexGen, and I will get you everything you need to win."

ARUN
(leaning in, intrigued) "And what's in it for you?"

SONAL
(voice filled with bitterness) "I told you, Mr. Sundaram. I want to finish off Vikram Oberoi."

ARUN
(pondering) "Okay, I'll give this a shot. But, I doubt if you know of ways to access

'classified information'. How long have you been working at NexGen?"

SONAL
(confidently) "A couple of months. And thanks to my job in the Admin department, I know a lot of Vikram's business associates. I know who he's meeting and where he goes to wine and dine them. I know when and why the bosses are making business trips. Most importantly, Vikram trusts me, and let's just say that he takes more than casual interest in me. For everything I don't know myself, I know of ways to make the right people in NexGen talk."

ARUN
(impressed) "Hmm… But, you'll need to make a lot of people talk. We need to first identify our marks – the ones who're vulnerable and most likely to give in to temptations… money, sex, whatever…"

SONAL
(nodding) "I've done my homework, Mr. Sundaram. I know our soft targets in NexGen."

ARUN
(smiling) "Good. But Sonal, you can't do this alone. I know of someone who can make the toughest of them go weak in their knees. Her name is Urvashi."

SONAL
(raising an eyebrow) "Urvashi?"

ARUN
(nods) "One of the most desirable escorts in town. She's worked for me a couple of times, when I've had to win over clients. She's really good at what she does. I'll give you her number. And I can pick up her bills for you. She can be quite expensive, you know."

SONAL
(looking thoughtful) "Alright."

ARUN
(leaning in, voice serious) "We need to lay down some rules of the game here, Sonal. We won't meet after today. Don't call me on my official number. I'll give you an unlisted number where we can be in touch. I hope you realize that, you're walking on thin ice here. Don't ever try to act smart with me. I don't easily forgive."

SONAL
(looking Arun straight in the eyes) "For me, it's not only about you, Mr. Sundaram. It's my mission at the end of the day."

ARUN
(smiling) "Well then, let's talk business. Have you heard of Evita?"

Act 53
Present Day

INT. VIKRAM'S LIVING ROOM - NIGHT

The room is dimly lit. The glow from the television casts eerie shadows. The news report is audible, and the camera focuses on the TV screen where SONAL is seen making her statement.

SONAL (on TV)
"I've lodged a formal complaint with the police against Mr. Vikram Oberoi for his prolonged sexual harassment."

Close-up on VIKRAM's face. He's visibly shaken, his face pale. He reaches for his phone and dials.

INSERT: PHONE SCREEN
"Sonal - Calling..."

The call goes unanswered. VIKRAM's frustration is palpable.

VIKRAM
(voice trembling)
"You fucking bitch!"

FLASHBACK SEQUENCE

Quick cuts of VIKRAM and SONAL in happier times. They're seen laughing on the bed,

VIKRAM making breakfast in the kitchen, and sharing intimate moments.

BACK TO PRESENT

VIKRAM's eyes are filled with tears, but there's also a hint of rage. He looks at the TV again, where SONAL's pixelated face is still visible.

VIKRAM
(smirking)
"I'm not going to let you do this to me, bitch! Vikram Oberoi is not going to be dragged away by a bunch of khakis."

INT. VIKRAM'S KITCHEN - NIGHT

Close-up on VIKRAM's hands as they frantically search through the drawers. He finds a sharp knife. He looks at it, a wicked smile forming on his lips.

INT. VIKRAM'S LIVING ROOM - NIGHT

VIKRAM returns to the sofa, pouring himself a drink.

VIKRAM
(laughing maniacally)
"One for the road."

He raises the glass in a mock toast to the TV, then downs the drink in one gulp. He looks at his left wrist, contemplating his next move.

VIKRAM
(whispering)
"Catch me if you can, bitch!"

With a swift motion, he cuts his wrist. Blood pours out. He laughs hysterically, the weight of his actions and the reality of the situation slowly sinking in.

CUT TO BLACK.

FADE IN:

INT. VIKRAM'S LIVING ROOM - NIGHT

The room is silent, except for the faint hum of the TV. VIKRAM's lifeless body is seen on the sofa, blood everywhere. The white leather upholstery of the sofa is stained with his blood, and the crimson lines flow down to the carpet.

Act 54

INT. PRESTIGE APARTMENTS - LOBBY - NIGHT

The wind howls outside, rustling the trees. The atmosphere is eerie. Police cars pull up, their lights flashing. The entrance of the building is grand, but tonight, it feels ominous.

INT. ELEVATOR - NIGHT

Several police officers wait inside the elevator. The button for the twenty-ninth floor is illuminated. The officers exchange glances, the tension palpable.

INT. VIKRAM'S PENTHOUSE - LIVING AREA - NIGHT

The door bursts open after a few attempts. The living area is dimly lit by the glow of the TV. The news bulletin shows VIKRAM's picture. The clock above the TV reads 8:55. The room is silent except for the hum of the TV.

The officers scan the room. They notice the whiskey bottle, the empty glass, and the magazines on the coffee table. The drawn curtains add to the gloom. The dining area and kitchen are visible in the distance.

The officers slowly approach the sofa. VIKRAM's lifeless body is sprawled on it, blood smeared everywhere. The bloody kitchen knife lies on the carpet near his feet.

INSPECTOR SALGAONKAR
(looking at VIKRAM's body, smirking)
"Tharki saala. The bastard ran away to hide inside his hole and called it quits escaping the prison. What an asshole!"

The other officers nod, some in agreement, others in disgust.

INSPECTOR SALGAONKAR
(philosophically)
"Look at him. This is what happens when you run after money... and women."

Another officer chimes in.

OFFICER
"Bad example for our kids."

The officers continue to survey the scene, the weight of the situation sinking in.

Final Scene

INT. NEXGEN - CONFERENCE ROOM - DAY

A large, modern conference room with a long table. The room is filled with the Department Heads of NexGen, all looking anxious. The atmosphere is tense. The large windows show the cityscape.

DEV
(standing at the head of the table)
"Gentlemen, these are difficult times for NexGen. Over the last few months, we've been faced with one disaster after another. And I don't want to blame any one person for the mess. It's our failure as a team. It's as much my failure as it was Vikram's."

The Department Heads nod in agreement, some looking down, others exchanging glances.

DEV
(continuing)
"In Vikram, I saw an extremely competent professional and entrusted him with the single most important position in the company. But, what I realized over time is that, the line between professional excellence and personal integrity is a thin one. The darkness you carry in the hidden chambers of your soul is bound to take in its grasp your conduct at the workplace. And that has got nothing to do with how smart or how learned you are."

The room is silent, everyone hanging on to Dev's every word.

DEV
(looking around the room)
"To make its way out of the crisis we are faced with today, this company needs a leader who is not just a visionary, but is someone who has demonstrated exemplary integrity and honesty, not just at work, but also off it."

The Department Heads look at each other, wondering who Dev is referring to.

DEV
(after a pause)
"And after much deliberation with my business partner Ashok, who unfortunately could not make it to this meeting as he is down with a flu, I have decided to hand over the reins of the India operations of NexGen to Ashwin Saxena."

The room erupts in applause. ASHWIN stands up, looking both surprised and proud.

ASHWIN
(voice filled with emotion)
"I'll try my best not to let you down, Dev."

DEV smiles warmly and walks over to ASHWIN. They shake hands and share a hug.

INT. NEXGEN - CONFERENCE ROOM - DAY

The room is filled with the Department Heads of NexGen. ASHWIN stands at the head of the table, with DEV beside him. The atmosphere is more positive now.

DEV
"So, Ashwin, what, in your view, should our immediate priority be?"

ASHWIN
"Dev, we've got a lot of bad press over the last few days. The clients are shaky. Our stock has hit rock bottom. We badly need a facelift."

He takes a deep breath.

ASHWIN
(cont'd)
"We will go to the media and reiterate our commitment to corporate ethics. With Rakesh Behl resigning, a couple of veteran technology practitioners will join us this week. This will increase our credibility. And then, we roll out some stunning new products. As quickly as we can. And for that, I'll need everyone's support."

He looks around the room, making eye contact with each Department Head.

DEV
(smiling)
"Sounds like a plan, Ashwin!"

The Department Heads nod in agreement, looking more confident.

DEV (cont'd)
"Back to work, boys!"

He heads for the door, with the Department Heads following him.

INT. COFFEE SHOP - DAY

SONAL and URVASHI sit across from each other at a table. They both have coffee in front of them. The atmosphere is relaxed.

URVASHI
"You know, Sonal, I've never earned more money in any assignment than this one. By the way, that geek in Tokyo was really hot! So was Vikram. Can't say that about the Systems guy, though."

They both laugh. SONAL then becomes more serious.

SONAL
(teary-eyed)
"You know, my mission would never have been complete without you."

URVASHI
(sincerely)
"I've often wondered why your mission was so important to you. But I never asked. And I won't ask today. But in all these years working for an escort agency, I've finally found a reason to feel proud. Thank you for that."

They both have tears in their eyes.

EXT. COFFEE SHOP - DAY

SONAL exits the coffee shop, looking content. She takes a deep breath, looking up at the sky.

SONAL
(voiceover)
"The police and the media now have all the videos. I'm the new darling of the media, an overnight celebrity. My story is all over the newspapers. Television channels are queueing up for my bytes. But none of these matters to me. What matters is that Rishi's death has been avenged."

She walks away, a satisfied smile on her face.

EXT. MARINE DRIVE - MORNING

SONAL stands looking out at the sea, lost in thought. The morning sun casts a golden hue on the water. The rush hour traffic is audible in the background.

SONAL
(voiceover)
"I wish Rishi were here to celebrate this moment with me."

A dreamy, ethereal version of RISHI appears, stepping out from the coffee shop. He waves at SONAL, running towards her with a big smile. RISHI reaches SONAL and they embrace, lost in each other.

SONAL
(voiceover, cont'd)
"I needed a lot of that, now that my battle is over."

The dream fades, and SONAL is left standing alone, looking out at the sea.

EXT. MANVI'S BALCONY - EVENING

MANVI sits with a cup of green tea, watching the sun set over the Arabian Sea. The world around her seems calm, but her face is etched with pain.

MANVI
(voiceover)
"My world has changed so much in the last few days. It seems that my life is now a series of tainted pictures."

She takes a sip of her tea, tears forming in her eyes.

MANVI
(voiceover, cont'd)
"It's not about Vikram's philandering or the scars in our marriage. It is not about the fact that, with the name of the family blemished forever, life looks uncertain for me and my little boy. It's about the sin I committed. Silently, shamelessly. Sending my conscience to sleep for months till the

media got tired of talking about it. It is about those moments of unpardonable indiscretion inside a hotel room a year ago, for which I will never forgive myself. It is about the young soul, bright and beautiful, that Vikram and I destroyed."

She looks down at her hands, remembering the events of the past.

MANVI
(voiceover, cont'd)
"Rishi Bhargav, a promising young boy. We snuffed out his flame, before it could light up the world."

A tear rolls down her cheek.

MANVI
(voiceover, cont'd)
"Have I suffered enough for my sins?"

The sun finally sets, casting the balcony in darkness.

FADE OUT.

THE END

www.ingramcontent.com/pod-product-compliance
Lightning Source LLC
LaVergne TN
LVHW041707070526
838199LV00045B/1239